Janice Kyle

Editor:	Janice Kyle, Inc.
Proofreader:	Barbara Phillips
Designed Cover:	Janice Kyle, Inc.
Digital Designed Cover:	Local Graphic Shop

National Library of Canada Cataloguing in Publication

Kyle, Janice, 1962-
Forbidden lovers caught in a web of lies, sex and deceit / Janice Kyle.
ISBN 1-55369-389-2
I. Title.
PS3611.Y44F67 2002 813'.6 C2002-901534-0

TRAFFORD

This book was published *on-demand* in cooperation with Trafford Publishing.
On-demand publishing is a unique process and service of making a book available for retail sale to the public taking advantage of on-demand manufacturing and Internet marketing. **On-demand publishing** includes promotions, retail sales, manufacturing, order fulfilment, accounting and collecting royalties on behalf of the author.

Suite 6E, 2333 Government St., Victoria, B.C. V8T 4P4, CANADA
Phone 250-383-6864 Toll-free 1-888-232-4444 (Canada & US)
Fax 250-383-6804 E-mail sales@trafford.com
Web site www.trafford.com TRAFFORD PUBLISHING IS A DIVISION OF TRAFFORD HOLDINGS LTD.
Trafford Catalogue #02-0202 www.trafford.com/robots/02-0202.html

10 9 8 7 6 5 4

Acknowledgments

I am giving thanks to my son Christopher for keeping out of my office during the development stages of my novel.

I am giving thanks to my friend Barb for her laughter and support.

I am giving thanks to my brother Vern who took time from his busy schedule to read my novel and for giving me encouragement. Big brother thanks for your commitment of not sharing my novel with anyone and much love is extended too you.

I am also giving thanks to my former Bosses for using the term, "Thinking Out Of The Box" during regularly scheduled business meetings concerning their goals and strategies. Over the years, I've incorporated this term into my personal life, which it has become the, "Plateau" for the creation of my novel. Creating this novel was certainly, "Thinking Out Of The Box," but this term has become the milestones for all future projects.

Author's Note

"Forbidden Lovers Caught in a Web of Sex, Lies, and Deceit," is a fiction erotica novel filled with explicit adult language. All names, places, and events are solely based upon the author's imagination and if by chance names, events, and places are reality, "It is strictly coincidental." The author is not insinuating; the wealthy sector of society has little or no morality but has written this novel exclusively for the purpose of adult entertainment. In addition, the author has substituted, "Pussey" for pussy.

Chapter One

A Weekend Getaway

On an extremely scorching and sun-drenched Friday, Carmen Hailey enjoyed the evening sunshine as she relaxed on her patio. She reminisced about her friends boasting on how beautiful Colorado Springs is during the summer months. She became so overjoyed until she could hardly control her thoughts on all the fun she could possibly experience during, "A Weekend Getaway to Colorado Springs." She enthusiastically debated with herself to why she should not fly away for the weekend but excitedly shouted out, "Why the hell not; I'm taking this trip, and I will have the best time of my life."

She immediately contacted her Travel Agency to make travel arrangements. She exhaled, "YEEEEES," the 7:00 A.M. flight Saturday morning will be perfect! But, I will prefer a late evening flight on Sunday. Okay Ms. Hailey, I will check to see what's available.

Ms. Hailey, there is a flight arriving in Seattle at 5:40 P.M. She moaned, "HMMMMMMMMMMM, is there a fight returning much later?" Sure, Ms. Hailey! There's a flight arriving at 2:00 A.M. Monday morning. Okay, the 2:00 A.M. return fight will be great! She thanked, the Travel Agent and dashed upstairs to pack. She responded, "Lets see! I will only be gone for the weekend, so there's no need to overly pack." She proudly smiled. This will be the best weekend that I've had in an awfully long time. Hell, I'm long overdue for a fun filled weekend! She packed an evening dress for a night out on the town, a swimsuit for relaxing at the pool, and a pair of jeans to return home in. "YEEEEEEEEEEEEEEEEEES," this is all I need for my weekend excursion. Oh, I should pack a few pairs of thongs. "I might not wear them, but I will pack a few pairs just in case."

Carmen awakened bright and early Saturday morning. She was so excited and determined not to miss her flight. She quickly showered, slipped into a pair of red shorts, a white low-cut sleeveless blouse, applied a small amount of makeup, and pinned her hair back with a brooch. She smiled as she glanced into the mirror and emotionally whispered, "I'm looking forward to this magnificent weekend." She loaded her overnight bag and removed the top of her red sports car. As she drove to the airport, she danced in her car seat and enjoyed the fresh morning air while singing her favorite songs. She parked her car and rushed inside. As she approached the ticket counter, the Agent replied, "Good morning Madam." Carmen blissfully said, "YEEEEEES, it's a great morning and surely to be a fantastic weekend!" The Agent handed her the ticket, "Gate A6, Ms. Hailey."

She thanked the Agent and leisurely walked to the gate. As she gradually turned the corner, she bumped into a tall and handsome man who appeared to be in an enormous rush. She stepped out-of-the-way and softly said, "Excuse me", but the man insisted, "No, it was my fault and please excuse me. I'm in a rush to get back to the ticket counter where I believe; I may have possibly left my wallet." She momentary looked him up and down thinking, "I would love to land at your destination!" She boarded the plane and found her seat in first class. The Stewardess announced the final boarding. Carmen sighed, "Great! I will have this seat all to myself." She looked intently out the window until she noticed someone sitting in the seat next to her. She glanced over to see who it was and detected the man she bumped into earlier. She became nervous and excited as a result of his appearance. She vigorously moaned and groaned to herself, "UUUUUUMMMMMMMMMMMMMMM."

Her heart thumped against her chest; but as usual she controlled her emotions. Whispering to herself, "I don't believe he's sitting next to me." She finally said, "Hello, didn't we bump into each other earlier?" Yes, we did! "Did you find your wallet?" Yes! Exactly, where I suspected it would be. "At the ticket counter." She smiled. "I'm happy you found your wallet. Especially, here at this busy airport! By the way, my name is Carmen." He whispered, "Such a lovely name." She slightly smiled. "Thank you!" Gosh Carmen! It's a pleasure meeting you. He extended his hand; "I'm Jack."

She became more and more excited as she talked with him. Her pussey became so uncontrollably wet until she thought; she would have an orgasm. She pressed her ass into her seat wishing, "Instead, it was his cock she was pressing against." She glanced at him and noticed his cock bulging in his pants. She closed her eyes and moaned delicately enough for him to hear her, "UUUUUUUUUMMMMMMMMMMMMM, AAAAAAAAAHHHHHHHHHHHHH." Literally, she wanted to fuck him on the plane. She whispered, "Your cologne smells, SOOOOOOOOO sexy." She thought, "How I would love to sit on his stiff cock?"

He passionately stared into her eyes, where is your destination? She lightly licked her lips and said, "Colorado Springs for the weekend." He touched her hand and said, "For business." She smiled. "No, I'm flying there for pleasure!" Carmen, you are my kind of woman. She responded, "Jack is your destination for business or pleasure?" Carmen, I'm flying to Colorado Springs for pleasure, just as you. He continued looking at her. "Where are you staying?" She smiled. "I'm staying at The Bed and Breakfast Cottage Inn on 6th and Madison." He shook his head; Yes, I have stayed there on several occasions. Excellent location! She exhaled, "Where are you staying?" He whispered, "With you!" She was stunned by his response and said, "Oh, you are!" He zealously laughed. "No, I'm simply kidding! I'm staying at a hotel six blocks from you." Carmen, why don't you cancel your hotel reservation, and stay with me this weekend? My hotel room has two queen size beds. Jack, that sounds like a great idea, but I really shouldn't! She moaned to herself; "My pussey is SOOOOOOOOO hot and wet. UUUUUUUUUMMMMMMMMMM, I would love for him to glide his tongue all over my body." He touched her arm, why don't you stop by my hotel room first to check things out before saying, "No!" She sighed, "Okay Jack, that sounds like an excellent plan!" She surprised herself upon making such hasty decision to stop by his hotel room. "Whenever she makes acquaintances with an unfamiliar man, she always engages in casual conversations to avoid revealing her secret fascinations."

When the plane landed, she thought, "What am I getting myself into this weekend? Hell, I will soon find out!" As they departed the plane, he said, "I have a rental car reserved for the weekend." Okay Jack, lead the way! He stopped before arriving at Williamson's Rental Car Agency – hugging her and whispering; "I would love to show you around town tonight." Jack, that sounds fantastic! As they waited in line for the rental car, she informed him, "I'm happy with my decision to fly here this weekend." He kissed her cheek, not as happy as I am. He signed for the car; I rented a fast, hot, red corvette for the weekend. She touched his arm and said, "Extravagance choice." Carmen, I knew you would say that. Jack, I always enjoy riding in a corvette; furthermore, I left my corvette parked at the airport. He hugged her before opening the car door. He got into the car, telling her; "You are beautiful!" He caressed her legs asking, "Do you care if I kissed you?" Yes, I do! Jack, why don't we wait until later? "Carmen, why not now?" She thought, "Why didn't I take the taxicab to the Bed and Breakfast Cottage Inn?" He responded, "I promise I won't bite your lips." She nervously laughed. "Jack, I know you will not bite my lips." She passionately touched his face as she slowly kissed his lips. She boldly moaned, "SSSSSSSSSSSSSSSSSSHHH, AAAAAAAAHHHHHHHHHHHHHHHH, OOOOOOOOOOOOOOHHHHHHHHHHH," as she slowly slid her tongue into his mouth. He was feeling extremely aroused from her kiss. He forcefully moaned, "SSSSSSSSSSSSSSSSSSHHHHHH, UUUUUUUUUUMMMMMMMMMMMM, AAAAAAAAAAAHHHHHHHHHHHHHH," Carmen, you feel tremendous. She gradually slid her tongue back and forth into his mouth, UUUUUUUUUMMMMMMMMMM, Jack. She embraced him incredibly close to her body. "AAAAAAAAHHHH, whatever fears she had earlier no longer existed."

She kissed his face as he held her in his arms. She firmly slid her tongue over his earlobe and than forcefully back and forth into his ear. He moaned, "SSSSSSSSSSSSHHHHHHHHHHHHHHH, UUUUUUUUMMMMMMMMMM, that feels GOOOOOOOOOOOOOOOOOOOOOD. Don't stop, AAAAAAAAAAAHHHHHHHH." He whispered, "Lets drive over to my hotel to check things out. I promise if you are not delighted with the room; I will drive you to wherever; you have reservations." Okay Jack!

While driving to the hotel, he asked, "Where is your husband or boyfriend this weekend?" Jack, "Do you believe if I truly had a husband or boyfriend, I would be here with you?" Carmen, I should hope not. So Jack, "Where is your wife this weekend?' He hesitated prior to responding. "She's at home. Yes! I'm married, but that doesn't stop me from being sexually attracted to another woman." No Jack, I can't sleep in your hotel room! "Carmen, why not? There are two queen size beds, and I promise; I won't force you into doing anything; you are totally against." Jack, you mentioned earlier you were flying here for pleasure. Yes! I'm here for pleasure and also to prepare for an upcoming meeting scheduled for Monday morning.

As he parked the car, he whispered, "Gosh! My cock is throbbing." He kissed her shoulder, please come check out the room. If you decide to leave, I will drive you to the Cottage Inn. Okay! I will check out your room. After checking into the hotel, the Desk Clerk handed Jack the keys and said, "Your room number is 1206. Sir, have a remarkable stay!" Jack stared at Carmen; I promise to show you an extravagant time this weekend, but you must relax and have fun. With a smirky smile on his face, he said; "I know that's why you are here, so you wouldn't be alone this weekend!" Now Jack, what make you believe that? "I'm here because I wanted to get away. All work and no play is making my life extremely boring!" Carmen, I know it's more to your visit here then what you are telling me. She caressed his back as the elevator door opened on the 12th floor. He squeezed her hand, lets check out room 1206. As he opened the door, she inhaled his cologne; "UUUUMMMMMMMM," he smelt wonderful.

He swung open the door and walked into the room and asked, "What is your opinion?" She smiled. "It's charming, Jack." He whispered, "This room has more than enough space for the both of us." He hugged her, "Will you stay here with me?" Jack, please give me a few minutes to consider your invitation. He walked over to her; let me help you make up your mind. He held her firmly in his arm and kissed her. Her heart raced from pure excitement. He whispered, "Baby, whatever you decide will be okay with me." She stared into his eyes as they kissed and knew right then; his room was where she wanted to spend her weekend. He asked, "Would you like to order a bottle of wine?" She moaned, "UUUUUUMMMMMMMMMMMMMM, that sounds excellent." She walked out onto the deck as he ordered the wine. When he hung up the phone, she returned inside the room asking, "Jack, aren't you planning to call your wife to let her know your flight arrived safely?" Sure Carmen, I will call her later. No Jack, please call her now, so she doesn't worry about you! "Trust me Carmen, my wife isn't at home worrying about me." Jack, you may possibly have problems in your marriage, but please call your wife out of common courtesy.

He dialed his home number but didn't get an answer, so he left a message letting Karen know; he arrived safely. He pulled her extremely closely too him and said, "You don't listen exceptionally well – do you! Karen isn't home worrying about me; we've been having numerous problems in our marriage over the past three years." She kissed him; I believe things can be worked out. Of course, Carmen, there's a possibility, but neither Karen nor I are doing anything to improve our marriage. Every possible chance I get, I leave town on business to avoid spending time with her. She doesn't seem to care about anything other than her created failing health problems. He placed his hands into his pocket. Shit! She isn't passionate about making love. He took her into his arms; I need sexual stimulation whether my wife needs it or not. He cheerfully laughed. "That's the nature of the raging bull." She laughed with poise. "Raging bull – what are you referring to?" He placed her hand on his throbbing cock and said, "This is my raging bull."

He caressed her back asking, "Will you make love to me?" Carmen, I will make it the best you've had! I realized you can't take my wife's position, but I haven't felt SOOOOOOOO sexually aroused in such a really long time. The only thing my wife ever does is complain about her failing health. Shit Carmen! I'm tired arguing with my wife about her health problem when I know there isn't a damn thing wrong with her. I want a woman who is spontaneous. My wife had every opportunity to fly here with me this weekend, but she decided to stay home. Her weekend will be spent complaining to her family about her failing health problems and about me not being sympathetic. Jack, I'm sure you have also contributed to your wife's problems. Carmen, you are right; I haven't always been there for Karen, but I can't change the irresponsible decisions; I have made in my past. He sighed, "I'm willing to do anything to perk up my marriage." So Jack, how often do you meet women at the airport and invite them into your hotel room? Carmen, please don't assume; it's customary for me to entertain women in my hotel room. I must admit; I was extremely attracted to you when I collided with you at the airport. I thought to myself; "It would be awesome spending time with her." After we were assigned seats together, I couldn't believe my fate.

Carmen, I promise; I won't pressure you into doing anything that you oppose. Whenever you decide, I will drive you to the Cottage Inn. I want you to trust me; I will never do anything to hurt you or mislead you. If there were any likelihood of my wife knowing about you, I wouldn't be asking you to stay here with me this weekend. She kissed his lips and moaned steadily, "EEEEEEEERRRRRRRRRR." I want to make love to you right now. "JAAAACCKKKKKKKKKK," she moaned as he kissed her lips. His cock was getting hard as a rock. He pressed his strong body extremely closely against her body. She passionately whispered in his ear, "UUUUUUMMMMMMMMMM,

Jack. I want to feel your cock stroking my pussey. AAAAHHHHHHHHHHHHHHH, SSSSSSSSSSSSSSHHHHHHHHHHH."

His breathing was getting louder and louder as he kissed her; sweat rolled down his forehead; his heart was pulsating against her chest, and his cock was throbbing against her body. He rubbed his hands back and forth over her back as she moaned and groaned, AAAAAAAAHHHHHHHHHHH. He excitedly whispered, "Carmen! OOOOHHHH, Baby, I want to fuck you SOOOOOOOOOOOOOOOOOOO badly. UUUUUUUUUUMMMMMMMMMMMM, I want to taste your PUSSSSSSSSSEYYYYYY."

She unbuttoned his shirt moaning, "OOOOOOOHHHHHH, Jack, you are so sexy." She kissed his lips as she unbuttoned and unzipped his pants. He whispered, "AAAAAAAAAAHHHH," as she stroked her hand back and forth on his big hard throbbing cock. UUUUUUUMMMMMM, Carmen. I want you to suck my throbbing cock. He moaned, "UUUUUMMMMMMMMMMMMMMM, AAAAAAAHHHHHHHHHHHHH." Take my cock into your mouth. I want to feel your hot mouth sucking my hard throbbing cock, "UUUUUUUUMMMMMMMMMMMMM,

OOOOOOOOOOOOHHHHHHHHHHHH, Baby YEEEEEEEEEEEEEEEEEEEES." Please suck my, "COOOOOCCCCCCCCKKKKKKKKKK." She knelt down, taking his big hard throbbing cock into her mouth. His cock was so hard until it pointed straight into the air like a lightening rod. She leisurely slid her tongue back and forth over his throbbing cock as he moaned, "OOOOOOOHHHHHHHHH, Carmen that FEEEEEEEEEEEEEEEEEEEEEEEEEELS SOOOOOOOOOOOOOOOOOOOOOOOO GOOOOOOOOOOOOOOOOOOOOOOOOD. UUUUUUUUUUUUMMMMMMMMMM, OOOOOOOOOHHHHHHHH, your mouth is so HOOOOOOT." She sucked his big hard throbbing cock as he moaned and groaned, "AAAAAAAAAAARRRRRRRRRRRRRR," in pure ecstasy. "OOOOOOOHHHHH," Baby, don't stop sucking my hard cock. Carmen, I want to stroke your pussey with my hard throbbing cock. She ignored him as; she bobbed her head back and forth while sucking his cock. He whispered, "SSSSSSSSSSSSSSSHHHHHHHHHHHH, AAAAAAAAAAAAAAAAAHHHHHHHHHH, don't stop sucking my cock." She squeezed her lips extremely tight around his cock. Shit Carmen! You are "SOOOOOOOOOOOOOOOOOOOOOOO GOOOOOOOOOOOOOOOOOOOD. Don't stop!" Carmen, "YEEEEEEEEEEEEEEEEEEES," your mouth is "SOOOOOOOOOOOOOOOOOOOO wonderful; I'm CUUUUUMMMIIINNGGGG. OOOOOOOHHHHHHHHHHHHHHH shit Carmen! I'm CUUUMMMIIIINNNGGG." She stopped fucking his cock. Practically out of breath he asked, he moaned, "OOOOOOOOHHH, why did you stop?" Please make me CUUUUMMMM. Oh Baby, your mouth is so HOOOOOOOOOT.

She was so excited! She escorted him over to the bed; he removed her blouse and bra dropping everything onto the floor. He slowly caressed her tits as she moaned, "OOOOOOOOOHHHHHHHHH, Jack." He knelt on his knees removing her shorts. "SSSSSSSSHHHHHH," he moaned as he firmly kissed her pussey. OOOOOHHHHHHHH, Carmen, you are SOOOOOOOOOOOOOOO sexy! He whispered, "I want to taste your PUUUUUUSSSSSSSEEEEEEEEYYYYYYYY. UUUUUUMMMMMMMM, I want to feel my hard throbbing rod stroking your pussey. SSSSSSSHHHHHHH, I can't wait to slide my cock into your HOOOOOOOTTTTTTTTT and wet steamy PUSSSSSSSEEEEEEEEEY."

He pressed his back against the bed as she sucked his cock. He vigorally slid his ass back and forth on the bed as he getting into the groove of having his cock sucked. "OOOOOOOHHHHHH,

Carmen, suck my cock. Baby, don't stop! Your mouth feels, SOOOOOOOOOOOOOOOOOOOO GOOOOOOOOOOOOOOOOOOOOOD. UUUUUUUUUUUUMMMMMMMMMMMMM, Baby, don't stop." She passionately slid her mouth faster and harder over his hard throbbing cock as he yelled, "Don't stop Baby. I'm CUUUMMMMMMMMMIIINNGGGG. Oh Carmen, I'm CUUUMMMIIIINNNGGGGG." She removed her mouth from his cock. He moaned, "AAAAAAAAAAAAAHHHHHHHHH, make me CUUUUUUUUUMMMMMMMMMMM." She intensely whispered, "I want to feel your hard stiff cock fucking my pussey. OOOOOOHHHHHH, Jack, fuck my PUUSSSSSEEYYYYYYYYYYYYY. UUUUUUUUUUUMMMMMMMMMMM, fuck me." He excitedly slid his body on top of her body then quickly slid his cock into her hot and juicy WEEEEEEETTTTTTTTTT pussey. He moaned, "OOOOOOHHHHHHHHH, Carmen, your PUUUSSEEEEEYYYYYYY is SOOOOOOOO hot! AAAAAAAAAAAAHHHHH, your pussey is GOOOOOOOOOD. SSSSSSSSSSSHHHHH, you feel so are WOOONNDERFUL." Shit Baby! Your PUSSSSSSSEEEEEEEEEYYYYYY is SOOOOOOOOO hot. AAAAAAAAHHHHH, my cock is throbbing."

Carmen and Jack rocked back and forth in bed getting their fuck groove on. Carmen yelled, "AAAAAAAHHHHHHHH, YEEEEEEEES, I'm CUUUMMMIIINNNGGGG." She whispered, "Don't stop fucking me, Jack. Your cock is making my pussey feel splendid. I'm CUUUUUUUMMMMIIIINNNGGG. Oh shit! Make me CUUUUMMMMM." Jack fucked Carmen harder and harder with his throbbing cock. She yelled, "JAAAAAAAAAAAAAACK, I'm CUUUUUMMMIIIIIINNNNGGGGGG." He was "SOOOOOOOOOOOOOOOO" excited; he could hardly control himself. He hadn't fuck so energetically in years. His cock was so hard; he moaned and groaned, "OOOOOOHHHHHHH, I'm CUUMMMIIIIIIIIINNNNGGGGG, AAAAAAAAHHHHHHHHHHHHHH, SSSSHHHSSSSSSSSSSSHHHHHHHH. Shit! I'm CUUUMMMMMMIIIIINNNINGGGG. SSSSSSSSHHHHHHHHHHHH, Baby, please don't stop. Take all of my CUUUMMMMMMM."

He held her tightly in his arms and said, "This was the best fuck I've had in a long time; I had forgotten how great it felt!" She rested in his arms while caressing his chest. As she kissed his lips, the phone ranged. She rolled over in bed asking, "Aren't you planning to answer the phone." He moaned, "SSSSSSSSHHHHHH," my cock is getting hard again. She whispered, "You really should answer the phone." He calmly answered the phone. Hello. Hi Karen, I'm doing fine and you. Yes, I arrived at 3:00 P.M.; I called when I arrived at the hotel and have been waiting for your call. "Where have you been?"

Carmen kissed his cock as he talked with his wife. He moaned, "UUUUMMMMM." Karen, I'm OOOOOOKKKKKKKAAAAAAAAAAAY. His cock was getting SOOOOOOOOOOOOOOO hard. He couldn't believe he was talking with his wife while getting his cock sucked by another woman. Carmen slid her hot mouth back and forth on his cock. He yelled, "OOOOOOOOHHHHHHH, Shit!" His wife asked, "Honey are you talking to me." Yes Baby! I'm talking to YOUUUUUUUUUUU. Karen, I wish you were here with me. We haven't made love in such a long time, and I miss holding you in my arms. Caressing your tits and kissing your pussey, "AAAAAAAAAAAAAHHHHHHHH;" YEEEEEEEEEEEEEESSSSSS, I enjoy fucking your pussey with my hard throbbing cock. I wish you were here right now sucking my hard throbbing cock, AAAAAAAAAHHHHHH. Karen, you know I love having my cock sucked. "Why don't you make love to me the way you use to?" SSSSSSHHHHHHH, you don't kiss me anymore; you don't embrace me in your arms. Shit Karen! I want to be love. "AAAAAHHHHHHHHHHH," I want to be fucked. Carmen slowly kissed his ball as he continued talking with his wife. He moaned, "OOOOOOOOOHHHHHHHHHHHH, my cock is so hard. Baby, your mouth FEEEEEEEEEEEEELS SOOOOOOOOOOOOO GOOOOOOOOOOOOOOOOOD; his voice was loud, "I love the way you are sucking my balls, SSSSSSSSSSSHHHHHHHHHH."

Carmen slid her mouth back and forth over his cock as he moaned, "Your tongue feels SOOOOOOOOOOOOOOOOOOOOOOOO GOOOOOOOOOOOOOOOOOOD." Carmen stopped sucking his cock and slowly slid her hot pussey over his cock. He moaned, "AAAAAAAAAHHHHHHH, I don't believe I'm being fucked." Karen interrupted asking, "Jack is everything all right there with you?" Yes Karen! I'm fantasizing about fucking your hot and steamy pussey. As he was losing control, he caught himself as he screamed, "CAAAAAAAAARRMMEEENNN. AAAAAAAAAAHHHHHHHHHHHHHHH, Karen, please don't fucking me. OOOOOOOOOHHHHHHHHHHH, Karen, I want you to fuck me. I want your love. OOOOOOOOOOOOHHHHHHH, I love fucking your pussey. I loved fucking your mouth. OOOOOOOHHHHHHHH, I need and want your love."

Karen asked, "Jack, what is happening with you? Are you talking to me?" Yes Karen! "I'm talking TOOOOOOOOOOO you. YEEEEEEEESSSSSS Karen, ride my cock. Make me CUUUMMMMM. Fuck me, Karen fuck me, AAAAAAAHHHHH. Don't stop! Ride my hard stiff cock. Karen, your PUUSSSEEEEEEYYYY is so hot and wet. OOOOOOOOHHHHHHHHHHHHHH, Baby, your PUUUUUSSSSSSSSSSSSSEEEEEY FEEEEEEEEEEEEEEEEEEEEEEEEEEEEEELS GOOOOOOOOOOOOOOOOOOOOOOOOD. Karen, I'm CUUUMMMMMIIIIIIINNNGGG. I'm CUUUUUUUMMMMMMMIIIIIINNGG. AAAAAAAAAAAAAAAAAAAHHHHHHHH. Damn! I'm CUUMMMMMIIIIIINGGGGG. I'm so excited KKKAAAAAARRRREEENNNNNNNN. Shit! You don't know HOOOOOOOOOOW GOOOOOOOOOOOD I'm feeling. My cock felt so wonderful sliding in your hot steamy pussey. AAAAAAAAAAAAAHHHH, OOOOOHH, Jack screamed as he CAAAAAAAAMMMMMMMED."

His cock was getting hard again. "OOOOOHHHHH, Karen, I can't get enough of your pussey. SSSSSSSSSHHHHHHHH, Baby, please fuck me; fuck me! OOOOOOHHHH, I want to fuck you." Karen listened as Jack moaned and groaned through the phone, "AAAAARRRR, SSSSSSSSSSSSSSHHHHHHHHH." She began feeling SOOOOOOOOOOOOOOOOOOOO horny. She removed her panties and slid her fingers back and forth into her wet pussey. Karen whispered in the phone, "OOOOOOOOOHHHHHHH, Jack, I want you now. I want you to fuck me. I can't wait until you get home. I want you to eat my pussey. "AAAAAAAAHHHHHHHHHHHH," Jack, I want you to fuck my pussey with your big hard throbbing cock." Karen slid her finger faster and faster in and out of her pussey. She moaned and groaned, "AAAAAAAAHHHHHHHHHHH, Jack, I want you to caress my tits. MMMMMMMMMMMM. Jack, my nipples are so hard"

"For the first time in years, Karen wasn't concerned about her failing health problems. She exposed her naked body as she caressed her tits and slid her ass back and forth on the bed getting into the groove of fucking herself with her finger." Jack, I wish you were here with me. He moaned, "EEEEEEERRRRRRRR, when I get home, I will fuck your PUSSSSSSSSEEEEEEEEYYYYYYYY until you scream for more and more of my throbbing cock."

Karen was getting into the grove of fucking her pussey with her finger; she was SOOOOOOOOOOOOOOOOOO excited until she didn't hear her husband whispering another women's name. Jack whispered, "Carmen, fuck me.

OOOOOOOOOOOOOOHHHHHHHH, your pussey is so GOOOOOOOOOOOOOOOD." Karen asked, "Who is Carmen?" He moaned, "Karen fuck your PUUUUUSSSSSSEEEEEEEYYYYYY with your finger. I know you are excited for me. AAAAAAAAAAAAAAAAHHHHHHHH, UUUUUMMMMMMM, I want you to make your PUUUUUSSSEEEEYYYYYYYYYYYYYYYY CUUUUUUUUUUUMMMMMMMMM." She slid her PUSSEEEEEEYYYYYYYY back and forth on her finger. She whispered, "Jack, I'm CUUUUMMMMMMMMIIIIIINNNGGGG, AAAAAAAAAAAHHHHHHHHHHHH, Jack, who is Carmen?" He moaned, "Please Karen, fuck your PUSSSSSSEEEYYYYYYYYYYYYY. I want you to CUUUUUUMMMMMMMM for me, Baby. Karen, CUUUUUUMMMMMM for your big daddy. OOOOOOOHHHHHHHHH, Shit! Carmen, I'm CUMMMIIIIIINNNIIIIGGGG. YEEEEEEEEEEEEEEEEEESSSSSSSSSSSSSSSES, Karen, I'm CUUUMMMIIIIIIIINNNGGGGG. SSHHHHHHHHHHHHHHHHHHHHHH." He was so excited until he didn't care what he yelled.

He knew he hadn't felt this GOOOOOOOOD in such a long time. He was finally being fucked the way he truly desired. YEEEEEEEEEESSSS, Carmen please make me CCUUUUUUUUUUUMMMMMMMMMMMMM.

AAAAAAAAHHHHHHHH, Baby, sweet Baby, I'm CUUUUMMMIIIIINNNNGGGGGG. Shit, I'm CUUMMMIIIIIINNNNGGGGGG. Karen moaned, "OOOOOOHHHHHH, Jack, I'm CUUUMMMIIIIIIINNNNNGGGGGG." Cum oozed from Karen's hot pussey as she moved her ass back and forth on her bed. She slid her hand back and forth over her clit moaning, "Jack, UUUUUMMMM. Jack, I came and it felt SOOOOOOOOO GOOOOOOOOOOD. Oh Jack, my cum felt GOOOOOOOOOOOOD." Karen continued sliding her ass against the bed telling Jack; "I can't wait until you get home; I want to feel your cock stroking my hot steamy PUSSSSSSSSSSEEEEEEEEEEEYYYYYYYYY. OOOOOOOOOOOHHHHHH, I can't wait to feel my HOOOOOOOOOOOTTTT and wet PUSSSSSSSSSEEEEEEEEYY sliding back and forth over your big hard throbbing cock."

Carmen showered while Jackson talked with Karen. "Over the years, he has yearned for compassion and love from Karen. He has done everything in his power trying to convince her how much he truly loved her but after many years of arguing and rejection; he's at the point of not caring if his marriage ended." She whispered, "Jack, I want and need you in my life; please forgive me for being unavailable to your needs. Over the past few years, I have been so absorbed in myself, until I have neglected your needs and desires. Jack, I truly want our marriage to work." His voice was unsympathetic. "Karen, I will no longer tolerate the arguing or your rejections. You have been complaining about your ill health over the past three years, damn, I can't continue living my life this way. How are you feeling today?" She hesitated before answering, "Not incredibly well. I have been in bed all day?" Karen, why didn't you answer the phone when I called earlier? Jack, I didn't feel up to talking with anyone. He became extremely quite, and later said, "Karen, I love you. I want and need someone to love me." He sighed, "It would be great if I could introduce new things into our marriage." I know you haven't been emotionally or physically well lately, but you really should seek professional counseling or our marriage is over. She began crying. "Jack, all I ever wanted was compassion from you concerning my illness. No! I wasn't feeling sick every day, but I thought if you believed I was sick; you would be more understanding toward my health."

She snappishly changed the subject. "You mentioned you wanted to introduce new things into our sex life. What types of new things?" He eagerly whispered, "OOOOOHHHHH, Karen, lets take our time, but I want to have sex with you and other women." She naively responded, "I don't understand what you are saying, Jack?" He hesitated before responding. "Karen, I want to bring new things into our relationship such as having threesomes. I want to fuck you and another woman at the same time! I know you will enjoy it. AAAAAAHHHHH, the sheer thought of fucking you and eating another woman's pussey brings chills down my spine." Karen whispered, "UUUUUUUMMMMMMMMMMMM, Jack, that sounds awfully freaky." Oh Karen, I know you will enjoy having threesomes. This will be the best fuck we have ever experienced. OOOOOOHHHH, Jack, I really don't know, "Let me consider this."

Carmen returned from the bathroom fully dressed. He glanced at Carmen and said, "Karen, I will call you later." He stared at her and promptly asked, "Why did you get dress?" Jack, I had a marvelous time with you this afternoon, but I would like to be driven over to the Cottage Inn. He walked over caressing her arm, UUUUUMMM, it's still early, and I really would like to enjoy the rest of the night with you – if you know what I mean. Yes! I know what you mean Jack, but I didn't fly to Colorado Springs to spend the entire weekend with you. Carmen, "Aren't you enjoying yourself?" Yes! I'm having a spectacular time with you, but there is a great deal more to experience here during this weekend. Carmen, I'm disappointed that you have decided to leave, but I understand. I will shower and drive you over to the Cottage Inn. Thanks Jack, but I will take a taxicab. No! I insist on driving you, also, I promised to show you the town.

Jack, by the sound of your conversation with your wife, it seems, as if you two haven't been intimate in years. "He glanced at Carmen but didn't respond." He later asked, "How can I keep in touch with you once you return to Washington? I promise; I will call you only twice a week!" He eagerly smiled. SSSSSSSHHHHHHH, Carmen, I would love to continue seeing you. She emphasized; "No Jack, it's wrong." Carmen, please consider my offer before saying, "No." I know you may sense I'm lying, but I'm really fond of you. I think, you are special, and I want to see you again and again. Carmen, I know you are also attractive to me. Jack, I have no interest in continuing this relationship with you because someone will eventually get hurt from our lies and deceit. Yes! I enjoyed my time with you but at no time do I want to pretend what we're doing is honest.

Carmen, I know the only reason you flew here this weekend – so you wouldn't be alone. Please tell me; this is true! No Jack, that's not true! I flew here this weekend for excitement. She sighed, "Yes Jack! I'm attracted to you and yes; I had an incredible time with you. You are fantastic in bed, but you are married and no, we shouldn't have fucked, but we did and Sweetie; it was great. Yes, I can fuck you again and again and never get tired of you, but we both know we will ultimately become, "Forbidden Lovers Caught in a Web of Lies, Sex and Deceit!" Carmen, call it what you like, but you are great, and I have enjoyed spending this time with you. Damn, I wish you could change your mind about you staying with me tonight. She smiled. "I promise; it gets better!" Jack, your wife will drop dead if she knew her husband is fucking an African American woman. Carmen, "What does color have to do with our relationship?" You are great! Shit, I have never fucked a pussey as hot as yours in my life.

Damn Carmen! Thinking about your pussey is making my cock – rock hard. I bet Jack! But, I would prefer staying at the Cottage Inn, so I can relax. Carmen, stay here at this hotel; I will pay for your room. Jack, money isn't the issue. Carmen, I promise; I won't disturb you. Jack please shower, and I will consider your offer. He showered and returned into the room undressed. She become extremely conscious to how sexy his body is. His complexion is slightly tanned, and his body is exceptionally toned. She moaned, "SSSSSSSHHHHH, Jack, you have done an excellent job keeping your body in shape." He smiled. So you like what you see! Jack, I really like what I'm seeing. Yes, I'm extremely attracted to you, but once this weekend is over, this fling is over. Carmen, lets not end our relationship because the weekend is ending; I believe fate brought you and I together. She irately laughed. "Jack, I don't believe fate happens to create dishonesty or to bring hurt and humility in anyone's life. Jack, you are in need of soul searching and; perhaps, you should seek to better understand the meaning of fate!" He seemed saddened by her remarks. So, you believe I'm dishonest. She walked over to the window. Yes, I believe; we are both being extremely dishonest, but will our dishonesty end here in Colorado Springs – I seriously doubt it will!

He walked over to her. Earlier, I discussed with Karen about introducing new things into our relationship, and I would like to introduce you to her. "For what reason, Jack?" He ran his hand through his hair, "AAAAAHHHHHHHH," I would love for you to have threesomes with Karen and me. Jack, you are out of your mind! No Carmen, I'm really serious! My wife isn't interested in making love, and I know having threesomes will truly arouse her. I don't think so Jack! You and your wife should seek professional counseling from a sex therapist. Sorry, I'm not a certified therapist. He sighed, "Carmen, threesomes will be awesome experiences for everyone involved. We will grow to want and need each other." No Jack, I'm not interested in your sick-minded ideas! Now, please get dress and drive me over to the Cottage Inn. He seemed angry, but he apologized, please forgive me; I should have waited until I knew you better. I wasn't thinking straight.

Jack, "How would I benefit from threesomes? I'm not desperate. I'm capable of meeting single men so don't assume you are giving me special treatment. I also hope you are not thinking; I'm lonely; therefore, I will to do anything for an incredibly good fuck. If you are thinking this, you are absolutely wrong. Trust me, I want no part of a threesome!" He hesitantly laughed. "Calm down before you go into cardiac arrest. It's not as bad as it sounds." He placed his arm around her. I was totally of out of character to ask you that question. My intentions were not to offend you, but it seems as if you would be open to almost anything. Yes Jack! I'm open to almost anything but not fucking another woman. He teased, "What about with me and another man?" Jack, you are sick but "HHHHHMMMMM – that sounds SOOOOOOOO enticing." They both laughed with pleasure.

He caressed her back as he kissed her neck. No Jack, I really should leave! He whispered, "Why don't you sleep in the other bed, and I promise to control myself." He unbuttoned her blouse and dropped it onto the floor as he energetically caressed her tits. She whispered, "You are not controlling yourself." He moaned, "UUUUUUUUUUMMMMM." She could feel his stiff throbbing cock pulsating against her leg. She kissed his lips; I have reservations at the Cottage Inn. Baby, please call to cancel your reservation. I know you want to stay here with me tonight, but you are too damn conceited to admit it. Jack, I didn't fly here to spend my entire weekend with you. Okay, if you really want to go, I will drive you there, but please have dinner with me first. She smiled. "Sure, dinner sounds great, and besides I'm getting hungry enough to eat your cock!" He adamantly laughed. "You are SOOOOOOOOOOOO much fun, and I'm really glad we met."

He glanced at his watch; there is an awesome Italian Restaurant on 5th and Taylor. I have eaten there on several occasions, and the food is magnificent; plus, the seating is romantically cozy. Jack, Italian food it shall be! She quickly changed into her black dress and a pair of black sandals. He kissed her forehead as he sized her up. How tall are you? She smiled and said," Six feet." He enthusiastically laughed. "That's what I thought – all legs. UUUUUUMMMM, you look extremely lovely." He opened the room door and said, "Lets go have a great time tonight; perhaps, I can convince you late about staying with me." And as promise, I will show you the town after dinner. He moaned, "AAAAAHHHHHHH, we will dance and come back to the hotel to fuck ourselves unconscious." She timidly laughed. "Everything sounds terrific except the fucking." He confidently laughed. "You know you want me and you can't get enough of me." That's true Jack, but we will see! As they walked into the parking lot, he held her hand and squeezed it extremely tight.

He opened the car door and hugged Carmen before she got into the car. He whispered, "You are stunning." Thanks Jack! He got into the car leaning over kissing her cheek. He whispered, "Thanks for this lovely day." They arrived at restaurant. As they entered the restaurant, the Waitress escorted them to their table. He handed them menus and said, "Please enjoy your meal." Jack teased, "And, after dinner as well!" The Waitress smiled as he walked away. Dinner was great! Just as, Jack paid the check; Carmen went into the ladies room to freshen up her makeup. When she returned to the table, he said, "The town is awaiting you, Madame."

Before he drove from the parking lot, he whispered, "How about kissing me for dessert." She kissed his lips. He moaned, "OOOOOHHHHHH, as she slowly slid her tongue into his mouth." He wrapped his arms around her moaning, "I would rather return to the hotel." No Jack, you promised to show me the town! Yes, but what about tomorrow before you leave out! No Jack! I want the see the town tonight, plus, the climate is magnificent. The stars are bright, and the night air is so fresh! Carmen, you are flying out on tomorrow; and perhaps, I may never see you again. We can always fly here again for a much longer stay. "SSSSSSSHHHHHHH," I want to embrace you in my arms all night. Drive Jack, the town is awaiting us! He took her hand and stroked his cock. "UUUUUUMMMMMMMMMMMMMM", Baby, I'm getting SOOOOOOOO horny. He unwaveringly laughed. "Too bad; we can't get into the back of the car for a quick fuck before seeing the town." She touched his arm; don't you ever get tired of fucking? He glanced at her. "Hell no, I was born to fuck!" Jack if your wife knew you are behaving in this manner; she would be really disappointed in your behavior. He inquired, "Are you psyche?" No Jack! But, I know she doesn't expect her husband behaving in this manner. He shook his head, Carmen, if my wife will not love me; I will seek affectionate from someone else regardless to how wrong it may seem.

Jack, I really feel sorry for your wife. He sounded angry, "Me too!" Hell Jack! Why don't you do something positive about your marriage? Well Carmen, it isn't that easy. Karen has visited many specialists regarding her failing health and the physicians can't find anything wrong with her. Jack, have you gone to the doctor's with her to provide moral support? No, my schedule doesn't allow me to drive all over creation with her! Please Carmen, I don't want to discuss this now – perhaps, some other time. You are really spoiling the mood of my stiff cock! She cheerfully laughed. "That's not my intentions, but you should seek professional help."

They drove through the city checking out the hot spots. The city nightlights were beautiful! He suggested, "Lets go dancing; I haven't dance in months." Well Jack, do you know of any Lounges? "Yes! Malcae Lounge, I was in town years ago and happened to run into an old acquaintance. He and I stopped in for cocktails. The music is lively, so I'm sure you will like Malcae." As they entered Malcae, he asked, "What is your opinion?" She smiled. "The music is lively as earlier stated; Jack, Malcae is where we shall dance!" They danced and laughed the night away. Gosh, Jack you are such as great dancer. Carmen, I'm getting old, so I must keep my bones active! Jack, how old are you? I'm fifty-six! UUUUUUUUMMMMM, Jack. You move like you are thirty-six and how do you get so much energy to fuck the way you do. Did you take some type of stimulant to boost your sexual drive without me knowing? Funny Carmen! Jack, don't be so sensitive. So Carmen, "How old are you?" Jack, ladies don't tell their ages. Oh, come on Carmen, "How old are you?" Lets see! I'm forty. Are you really Carmen? Yes, and I know; I don't look one day over twenty! He cheerfully laughed and said, "And, extremely conceited I might add." Jack, I'm not conceited; I'm simply being honest. I have worked exceptionally hard maintaining my looks, so I'm enjoying how good I look and feel. Carmen, I'm only joking, you look terrific. Thanks

Jack, but I know. He energetically laughed. "Your modesty doesn't conceal your conceitness." He laughed again. "Ms. Conceitness are you ready to leave." Sure Jack. Thanks, I've had an excellent time tonight! He had a smirky look on his face. Great, and there is more to come! Such as what, Jack? He kissed her, SSSSSHHHH; we will end the night with sensational fucking. Jack, "Aren't you tired?" He smiled. "No, my sexual stimulant has reactivated!" She vigorously laughed. "You are too funny." He caressed her leg; this is phase II. Jack, I'm tired and really would like to rest. Carmen, are you telling me you can't handle my cock. She impulsively laughed. "No, I'm not saying that, but you do have a stallion!" He slightly laughed. "You can recuperate once you return to Washington."

He divulged, "You haven't told me anything about your husband or boyfriend." She shook her head, "I don't have a husband, but I have been occasionally dating Jessie Hopkins. We don't see much of each other because of his busy schedule. He has been overly zealous in achieving his goals of climbing the corporate ladder. I must admit, he has done extremely well for himself; but he never seems to find time to enjoy the pleasures of life." Carmen, is Jessie married? Jack, are you implying that I have a practice of sleeping with married men. No Baby! I'm only asking a question. No Jack! Jessie is single. His wife passed away four years ago, and he has since buried himself in his work. Jack sarcastically said, "So Jessie buried himself in his work rather then burying his cock inside a steamy hot pussey. Carmen, I don't believe he's being honest with you." Gosh Jack, not everyone thinks about fucking as much as you! Carmen, is anything wrong with that? She happily laughed. "No! Fucking is amazingly awesome. Jessie has asked me to spend more time with him, but I'm also extremely busy establishing a solid foundation business, in efforts, of creating a successful business." Carmen, is he white? No! Jessie isn't white; he's dark, tall, and remarkably sexy. So Carmen, he's black? No Jack! He's African American. Same thing. No Jack! He's African American. Okay, I stand corrected!

He caressed her leg. Carmen have you made up your mind whether you are staying with me tonight? There is an extra bed in my room. If you are tired, we can rest. Yes Jack! I will stay in your room tonight, but only under those conditions, "That, I sleep in the extra bed." He parked the car and kissed her lips. He whispered, "Lets try something." No Jack! I'm awfully tried, so please stop. Okay Carmen, lets go inside. He leaned over and kissed her neck. She moaned, "AAAAAAAAAAAAHHHHHH." He slid his tongue into her mouth. She caressed his face as he moaned, "SSSSSSSSSHHHHHHHHHHHH, you are making me feel SOOOOOOOOOOOOO horny." He unzipped his pants and removed his cock. UUUUUUUUMMMMMMMM, she stroked his cock exceedingly slowly. She whispered, "No! We should stop in this parking lot." Come on Baby relax, no one will see us. She stroked his cock as they kissed. His breathing was loud. He moaned, "AAAAAAAAAHHHHHHHHHHHHHHH, SSSSSSSSHHHHHHH, as breathing streamed up the car windows." Voices approached the car. No Jack, stop! Someone will see us. He moaned, "UUUUUMMMMMMMM, shit don't stop!" No Jack! He moaned, "SSSSSSSSSSHHHHHHH, don't stop Baby!" She insisted, Jack lets go upstairs; I mean it! He acknowledged, "Okay; I'm being selfish; let's go upstairs." She said, "I sense; you are totally out of control, or you have lost your mind." He zipped his pants, no Baby; I haven't lost my mind; perhaps, a little out of control.

As they rode the elevator, he persuasively said, "Please don't be angry with me." As the elevator door opened, she said, "Jack, you can never make me angry." They entered the room; she walked over to the bed. As she rested on her stomach with her eyes closed, his hand caressed her back, but she was too tired to ask him too stop. He unzipped and removed her dress. He slid his tongue over her tits and robustly encircled her nipples. She moaned mightily as he sucked her breast, "AAAAAAAAHHHHHHHHHHHHHHH."

He effectively slid his tongue over her pussey taking his fingers slightly opening her pussey. He slid his tongue over her clit. "AAAAAAHHHHHH," she whispered, "Jack, your tongue feels SOOOOOOOOOOOOOOOOOOOOOOOO GOOOOOOOOOOOOOOOOOOD. Jack, please don't stop eating my pussey. Jack slowly slid his tongue into her pussey. Shit Jack! I'm CUUUUMMMMMMMMIIIIINNNGGGGG. AAAAAAAAAAHHHHHHH, Jack, please don't stop! Make me CUUUUMMMMM." He slid his body on top of her and placed his cock into her pussey. He moaned, "AAAAAAHHHHHHHHHHH, shit Carmen! Your pussey is SOOOOOO hot." She moved her ass back and forth on the bed as he fucked her with his extremely huge and magnificent cock. "Fuck me Jack, and please don't stop!" Ring, ring, he sighed, "Damn!" Carmen asked, "Aren't you planning to answer the phone; perhaps, it's an emergency." He answered, "Hello. Hi, Karen is everything okay." Yes Sweetie! I miss you very badly. I want us to finish where we left off on yesterday. Karen, it's 5:25 A.M in the morning. I'm resting, so I will call you later in the day.

She caressed his legs as she shook her head and whispered, "Go-ahead – make Karen cum again." Jack said, "Okay, Karen, I will make you CUUUUUUMMMMMMMMMM." Carmen rested on her back as Jack kissed her. Karen asked Jack, "Sweetie what are you doing to me?" Karen, I'm kissing your lips passionately. I'm sliding my tongue down to your tits. Baby, I'm slowly and passionately sucking your nipples. Karen was breathing in the phone "AAAAAAAAHHHHHHHHHHH." Jack, don't stop! What else are you doing to me? Karen, I'm sliding my tongue down to your PUSSSEEEEEEEEY and slowly licking your clit. Carmen slid her clit back and forth over his chest. She wanted to scream out his name, but didn't want Karen hearing her screams of ecstasy, so she controlled herself. She strongly moaned, "Jack, your tongue feels so GOOOOOOOOOOOOOOOOOD." He moaned, "UUUUUUUUUUUMMMMMM, Karen, take your finger and rub your clit, and move your ass back and forth on the bed. YEEEEEEEEEESSSSSSSSS, go ahead fuck yourself with your finger." Karen moaned and groaned, "OOOOOOOOOHHHHHHHHHHHHHH, Jack; my PUSSSEEEYYYYYYY is so hot and wet. I want to feel your big hard stiff cock fucking my pussey." He whispered, "I'm fucking your hot wet pussey", but instead slid his hard throbbing cock into Carmen's pussey. Gosh! Jack was so horny. He moaned, "I'm fucking you, Karen." Carmen moaned and groaned, "AAAAAAAAAAAHHHHH." He screamed out, "Carmen's name. hot." Karen screamed, "OOOOHHHHHHHHH; I'm CUUUMMMMIIINNNGGGGG." Jack screamed, "Go on Baby and CUUUUUUMMMMMMMMMMMM for your big daddy." Karen screamed, "Yes! I'm CUUUUUUMMMMMMIIIINNNGGGG for you big daddy." Suddenly, Carmen screamed, "AAAAAAAAAAAAAHHHHHH, Jack, I'm CUUUUUMMMMMIIIIIINNNGGGGG. AAAAAAAAAAAAAHHHHH. Jack, Jack, Jack, I'm CUUMMMMIIIIIIIINNNGGGG." Karen breathing was getting louder. She screamed; "I'm CUUUMMMMMIIIINNNGGGGG." She relaxed her body on the bed. Shit Jack! I'm CUUUUMMMIIIIIINNNNGGGG, but Jack wasn't really listening to Karen. He was to busy getting into the groove of fucking Carmen's hot, steamy, and wet pussey. He moaned, "Karen, Baby." Yes Jack! Karen, Baby. Yes Jack! Baby, I'm CUUUMMMIIIIIIIINNNGGGGG. Karen, Baby, your pussey felt so amazing.

Karen whispered, "Thanks Jack. I will see you when you get home. I can't wait until you get home on Tuesday!" I know Baby; I can't wait either. Bye-Jack. Bye-Karen. He thanked her and said, "Gosh! I never thought I would experience this in my wildest dreams, and I can't wait until the three of us are together." She said, "Not on this life Jack, perhaps when we meet in hell." He laughed as he rolled over onto his back as she fell asleep in his arms.

Carmen awakened and softly said, "Jack its 1:45 P.M. lets shower and dress." Baby please relax, I'm awfully tired. "Okay Jack, one more hour." The phone ranged. Oh no Jack, not Karen again! I will not help you make her cum. Jack, you are on your own. He answered the phone. Hello. Hi Karen. Sorry Baby, I'm walking out the door to attend a meeting, so I can't talk right now. Yes! The meeting is scheduled for Monday, but we are preparing for it today. I will call you later. I promise. I love you to Karen. Bye-Baby. Karen moaned, "UUUUUMMMMMMMMMM, Jack, I'm exhausted. Bye-Jack."

Carmen caressed his chest. Gosh Jack! It seems as if Karen is having an extraordinary time. What an astonishing prescription to enhance your relationship with her! Yes Carmen! Karen and my relationship is missing excitement. Carmen glanced at the clock. Jack, its 2:45 P.M., lets go lay out by the pool; that sounds like a marvelous idea. We can order something to eat down by the pool. He rested in bed with an erection. No Jack! Lets go outside and relax at the pool. He squeezed her arm, damn Carmen, I want you! Instead, they showered and slipped into their swimsuits and headed for the pool. Many people were at the pool having a lazy Sunday afternoon. UUUUMMMM, Jack, the sun is beautiful today!

She sighed, "This is a great spot to relax – let's stop here." She asked, "Would you like to order something? I'm getting extremely hungry." He laughed with pleasure. "You are always hungry." True Jack, I'm always hungry for food, and you are always hungry for pussey. "Which is worse?" He cheerfully laughed. "A man can't live without great food or an incredibly hot pussey." He ordered a turkey club and she ordered a large oriental salad. While waiting for their meal, Carmen said, "Jack, I don't know your last name." Oh, you are right. 'It's Harper. Jackson Harper. She extended her hand, please to meet you Jackson Harper. Mr. Harper, I'm Carmen Hailey. He passionately said, "It's a pleasure meeting you, Ms. Carmen Hailey." Carmen, do you have any children? No children, Jack! Jack, do you and Karen have children. Yes! Karen and I have three, a son twenty-five, a son thirty, and a daughter twenty-six. So, have they all left the nest? Yes! They are all married. I hope; they are not following in their father's footsteps. He frowned, "What do you mean by that?" Use your imagination. Okay Carmen, I get your point!

He stared into the sky, Carmen, have you thought about flying out on Tuesday? No Jack! I really must get back. It would be nice if I could, but I can't. We can always meet in a couple of months. Please, Carmen stay longer. No Jack, I really can't! My business partner is expecting me on Monday, and

Jessie is also expecting me. He has a surprise for me. "Can't you call to let him know, you will be returning on Tuesday?" No Jack! I'm not calling Jessie – if I wanted to spend my weekend talking with him; I would have stayed home. Any ideas to what his surprise might be? No Jack! But, when I find out; I will let you know. He smiled. Perhaps his surprise is an awesome old fashion fucking. Jack, you are too funny, but that's not a bad plan. My pussey is becoming addictive to an incredibly good cock. Thanks to you, Jack! He laughed anytime Carmen. Who is your business partner and what kind of business do you operate? Jack, we can discuss my business affairs on a later date.

He rested his head against his chair, how did you meet Jessie? She stared at him without responding. Carmen will you please answer my question. Sure Jack! I meet Jessie a few years before his wife passed away. I had no interest in him because I knew he really loved her. They were high school sweethearts married for thirty-five years. Shit Carmen! That's a long time to be with one woman. Not really Jack! If you truly love someone, time isn't relevant. I would hope those are your plans with Karen but after this weekend; your behavior frightens me. He boldly laughed. "Yes Carmen, those are my plans but hell, it's really hard to know for sure!"

Is Jessie my age? Gosh Jack! You are extremely inquisitive. He' sixty-two years old! Carmen, he's too old for you. No wonder, you two haven't had sex in a while! "He is lacking sexual stimulant." Oh, Jack stop it! I never mentioned to you; I haven't had sex in a while. Damn Carmen! Jessie is twenty-two years older than you. So Jack, you are sixteen. You are right, Carmen! But, you know I can give you a mind-blowing fuck any day. She happily laughed. "So it seems." Hopefully, Jessie doesn't disappoint you when you two are finally together. Now Jack! You are more conceited than I am. No Carmen, once a woman has encountered a mind-blowing fuck, she doesn't want to waste her time on someone who can only fuck for fifteen minutes or less and fall asleep! She joyfully laughed. "That's true! But, I suspect Jessie can last longer than fifteen minutes." He blissfully laughed. "Will you tell me how long, after you have fuck him?" You are sick, Jack. No, only curious! You seem a little afraid; you might have competition? He delightfully laughed. "As I said earlier Carmen, I'm curious."

I asked you earlier Carmen; would you participate in a threesome, and you said, "No!" What about a foursome?" Gosh Jack! I'm seriously beginning to question whether you have any morality at all. Hopefully, your occupation doesn't involve dealing with many women – if so they are in serious trouble. I wouldn't be surprise if you don't have numerous harassment charges filed against you. Carmen, never on my or your life! I'm too smart for that! Carmen, I am a genuinely professional man. Jack, what is your occupation? He enthusiastically smiled. I'm an extremely prominent attorney, but I'm not here to discuss my business success with you. She smiled. You are revealing your conceitness. He confidently laughed. "It's contagious."

Carmen don't worry; I'm only testing your reactions when I mention having a threesome. Jack, how do you judge my reactions? He laughed without a care in the world. "You are a prude." Now Jack, you know Karen isn't willing to have a threesome. Sure, she would! Baby, Karen does anything I ask of her. Jack, not anything! She didn't stop pretending to be ill although her physicians haven't found anything wrong with her. He anxiously laughed. "Sure she will, I only have to ask." Jack, you are so full of bullshit. He removed a picture of he and Karen from his wallet. Carmen stared at the picture; she's really beautiful." Yes Carmen! She is beautiful. Carmen, I'm being truly honest with you; Karen has given me permission to sleep with any woman that I have desires for – but never bring her home.

Jack, then, why in the hell are you talking about a threesome? Because, I know I can change her mind. Jack, the only mind needs changing is your own. He smiled. "Lets drop the subject Carmen. I may change your mind; one day really soon." She glanced at her watch. "What's taking our food so long to get here?"

The Waitress returned and apologized for the long wait. He cleared his throat; it has been busy all day. "Thanks Jack, the meal was terrific!" He demanded, "Lets go upstairs and fool around; you are making me feel horny wearing that swimsuit." Jack! I'm not having any more sex with you this weekend. I want to go outside to enjoy the sunshine; perhaps, it may be raining when I return to Washington. UUUMMM, my cock will bring abundance of sunshine to your pussey. They both laughed without a care in the world. "You are right Jack; your cock is an awesome treat. You can say your cock brings sunshine to my pussey." He smiled. "Carmen, I know it does – simply by your moans and groans." Carmen, let go upstairs; we can come back later. I want to shower with you. Gosh Jack! Please control your cock. I can't Carmen; I want to fuck you. Okay Jack, you have twisted my arms. Lets go upstairs! Thanks Baby.

They entered the room. Jack said, "I will start the shower, Carmen." He stood in the restroom waiting for her. He yelled, "Baby, the water is ready." She walked into the restroom. He moaned, "Oh Baby, I can't wait to feel your body against mine." She softly whispered, "OOOOOOOHHHHHHHH Jack, the water feels GOOOOOOOOOD." He kissed her and said, "Yes Baby! It does feel GOOOOOOOOOOOOOOOD." She kissed his lip as the water pound against their bodies. She took the soap and lathered it into her hands and vigorously stroked it over his chest. His cock was getting really hard. She lathered soap on his throbbing cock as she caressed it with her slippery hands. She detained the soap in her hand as she caressed it against his cock. He moaned. "AAAAAHHHHHHHH. Carmen, UUUUUMMMMMMMMMMMMMM, this feels GOOOOOOOOOOOOOOOOD." She continued lathering the soap against his hard stiff cock as he moved his cock back and forth in her hand. He groaned, "SSSSSSSSSSSSSSSSSHHHHHH, AAAAAAAAAAAAHHHHHHHHHHHHHH." Jack's body trembled from excitement. He moaned and groaned, "AAAAAAAARRRRRRRRRR," as she rested her body against his body. Jack, I need to get dress, I don't want to miss my flight. UUUUUMMMMMM, I wish I could change your mind to stay until Tuesday. He held her head as he ran his hand through her hair. He kissed her; she could feel his cock getting hard. He turned her face toward the wall. He slowly kissed her back as he slid his stiff cock back and forth into her pussey. She screamed, "OOOOOOOOOHHHHH, Jack, that feels SOOOOOOOOOOOOOOOO awesome. AAAAAAAAAAAAHHHHHHHHHHHH. YEEEEEEEEEEEEEEEEEEEEEES. Jack make me CUUUUUMMMMM." His was breathing incredibly hard. He fucked her pussey faster and faster. The slapping sounds of their wet bodies were echoed the bathroom. "AAAAAAHHHHH, Jack, please don't stop! Shit! Don't stop fucking my pussey please make me CUUUUUUUUUMMMM. YEEEEEEEEEEEEEEEEEEEREEEEEEES, Jack, I'm CUUUMMMIIIIIIIIIIINNNGGGGG. AAAAAAAAAHHHHHHHHHHHH." Jack moans were getting amazingly louder and louder, "CARMEEEEEEEEEEEEENNNNNNNNNN, OOOOOOOOOHHHHHHHHHHHH, CARREEEEEEEEENNNNNNNNNNNNN, Oh shit! I'm CUUUMMIIIIIIIIINNNGGGG. AAAAAAAAAAAHHHHHHHHHHHH, Baby, Baby, Baby that felt GOOOOOOOOD!"

They finished showering and returned to the bedroom. It's getting late; I will get dress so you can drive me to the airport. Shit Carmen! I wish you would change your mind about staying. No Sweetie! I told you earlier; Jessie has made plans, and I really should get back to my boutique. Liz, will worried if I'm not there first thing Monday morning. If she calls my home and doesn't get an answer, she will be somewhat concerned about my whereabouts. He sighed, "Baby, call Liz and tell her; you are out of town until Tuesday." Jack, I must leave tonight, but I had an amazing weekend. Hopefully Carmen, I will see you when we both return to Washington! "UUUUUUMMMMM," you haven't told me how

I can get in contact with you. That's true Jack. I really don't believe; it's a good idea to continue this "Forbidden Love Affair."

Carmen, why don't you call Jessie to let him know that you are changing your travel plans. No Jack! I'm not canceling Jessie's plan. He sighed, "Will you call him to find out whether he has made plans?" Okay Jack, you have twisted my arms. I will call Jessie. She dialed his home hone number. Hello Jessie, it's Carmen. "How are you tonight?" No! I'm still in Colorado Springs. My flight leaves out within the next hour. Yes Jessie! I had a fabulous time this weekend. "How was your weekend?" Carmen, I worked; I had tons of deadlines to meet. Jessie, I should have guessed you spent your weekend at the office. She asked, "So is my surprise still planned for Monday?" He laughed with conviction. "Carmen, you know that I'm a man of my words." She asked, "Will you give me a hint, or should I wait until Monday?" He didn't respond. Okay, I will wait, but I look forward to my surprise on Monday. "What time?" 6:oo P.M., okay, I will be ready! OOOOHHH, you are sending someone to pick me up. "Is he sexy, or should I wait to engross myself in your sex appeal?" She laughed. "I thought you might say that." Bye-Jessie! I will see you on Monday evening. Yes Jessie! I met some extraordinarily fascinating people this weekend. She hesitated, I had an experience; I thought would never be possible. Bye-Baby. She hung up the phone. Sorry Jack, I must return tonight; Jessie has made plans, and I don't want to disappoint him, since he has gone through the trouble of making these plans. Plus, he said, "He miss me and wish; I was there with him." Jack frowned; "I don't need to hear that much detail." She bashfully laughed. "Do I hear a sign of jealousy?" He walked over to the door; no, you don't detect jealousy, but I will miss you very much, also.

He glanced at his watch; will I ever see you again? If you would like Jack, but not on a regular basis after all you are married. I really would like to start a relationship with Jessie. Shit Carmen! Don't remind me! But what does my marriage or Jessie have to do with you and me starting a relationship. She sighed, "A lot Jack! Please sincerely consider not pursuing this so call relationship between us because it will only create mistrust. He appeared extremely angry. "Carmen, I don't believe you are saying these things; you didn't seem concerned about broken trust when we met on Saturday." You are right Jack; I flew here this weekend in pursuit of having a spectacular time and my mission has been accomplished. Now, it's time for us to return to our routine lifestyles. Jack, we fulfilled our fantasies and Sweetie, all fantasies must come to an end. He rubbed his hand through his hair. Hell! I sure wished it didn't have to end so quickly. Jack, I said earlier we could still see each other on frequent occasions. Perhaps, dinner once a month! He excitedly laughed. "How about dinner and a first-rate old fashion." She abruptly stopped him." No Jack! He kissed her cheek. I promise; I will not drink my sex stimulating juice. She suspiciously laughed. "What's sex-stimulating juice?" He laughed at the top of your voice. "That's top secret."

Jack, will you please drive me to the airport? Yes Carmen, are you ready? "Will you please leave me your home phone number?" As long as, you don't call me to frequently. "What about your address?" No Jack! I'm not giving you my home address because you are not welcome to visit under no circumstances. Okay Carmen, your phone number is sufficient for now. He wrote her phone number down. He stared at the number and said, "Thanks Carmen! Would you like my phone number?" No Jack! Are you crazy, I don't want your home number? No Baby! This is my number at my office. She sighed, "Sure, I will call you occasionally to see how things are with you." He smiled. "What about calling to make a date for a good quality fuck?" She shook her head. There you go again, Jack. He smiled at her. "I'm only kidding!" She touched his arm. I know Jack, and I really like your sense of humor.

He picked up her overnight bag and said, "Baby, let's leave before you miss your flight." He sat the bag down and said, "That sounds so tempting." I don't think so Jack. We have one hour to arrive at the airport so don't try any funny business and besides the airport is only twenty minutes away. Shit Carmen! I really hate seeing you leave. "So Jack, what if I didn't meet you at the airport – would you have been alone or would you have met someone at a lounge or at the hotel pool?" He nervously laughed, "I would rather buy a magazine and masturbate." You are the first woman; I have spent time with during a business trip. She blissfully laughed. "Really Jackson! Should, I feel privileged?" He looked intently at her; don't call me that – I prefer Jack. She smiled. "Okay. I will call you, Jack."

Carmen, you may believe that I'm lying, but I'm starting to have enormous feelings for you. She hastily responded, "Come on Jack, you have been with me for only thirty-five hours; therefore, it's extremely difficult for you to cultivate intense feelings for me." He sighed, "I'm serious Carmen." She passionately affirmed, "You are infatuated with my hot, brown, wet, steamy pussey." He intensely laughed. "Carmen, don't joke around when I'm being serious." She cleared her throat. Okay Jackson, I will be serious, but I know you don't have strong feelings for me. She acknowledged, "I prefer Jackson; she moaned, "SSSSHHHHHH," Jackson sounds so intriguing!" The next time we make love, I will scream, "Jackson, fuck me, AAAAAAAAAAHHHHHH fuck me."

He vigorously laughed. She reframed from laughing. Jack, stop laughing, "I'm serious." Baby, I can't wait to hear you scream, Jackson. He stroked his cock; you have enough time to practice now. No! I will not miss my flight. Okay, are you ready? Sure Jackson, I'm ready! As they drove to the airport, she relaxed her head against the car seat. She touched his leg and said, "We must do this again really soon." He squeezed her hand. "All I need to know is when and where!"

Upon giving her ticket to the Ticket Agent, he responded, "Sorry Ms. Hailey, there is a one hour delay." She angrily responded, "Are you sure?" Yes! Ms. Hailey – one-hour delay! The pilot became ill, so we must wait for a replacement pilot. He will be arriving on the 12:10 A.M. flight from Kansas. Carmen yelled, "Oh great!" Jack whispered, "Calm down, this means we can spend more time together." She smiled at him. "How did, I guess you would say that?" He caressed her back. Lets go back too the hotel, and I will bring you back within an hour. He suggested, "You have time now to scream, "Jackson." No Jackson! I'm staying here at the airport. Why don't you return to the hotel to get a few hours of sleep? You have a long day ahead of you. She sighed, "What time is your meeting?" He placed his hands into his pockets. My meeting is scheduled at 9:00 A.M. Gosh Jackson! I'm so sorry. Why don't you leave and get some rest? No Carmen! I'm staying here until your flight leaves.

Okay Jack, but you will be unhappy later in the day for making this decision to stay here with me. Baby, I can get rest when I return from the meeting.

Lets take a walk through the airport. Oh, Jackson everything is close! I know; we can find a quite location to make out. "Jackson not here at the airport." Have you ever fucked at an airport? "No, I haven't!" He smiled. Lets make tonight a new experience for the both of us. Come on Jackson! I'm starting to get horny. Don't you think Jackson; we are acting out of control! He licked his lips. No! We are acting like horny adults who want to fuck. "AAAAAAAAAAAHHHHHHHHHHHH," lets find a location so we can kiss and if we fuck, we fuck. Okay Jack, lets find a quite location. They walked until they find an empty shoeshine station out of the public's view. He jerked her arm; let's stop here. This is a perfect location! She nervously laughed. "You are right Jack, this location is a perfect location!" She whispered, "Jackson; I'm kissing your lips, your nose – she kissed his nose softly, your eyes – she kissed his eyes softly, your cheek – she kissed his cheeks softly." He was feeling extremely excited. He moaned exceedingly loudly, "UUUUUUUMMMMM, SSSSSSSSSSSHHHHHHHHHHHHH." She unbuttoned his pants and firmly stroked his cock as he moaned, "EEEEEERRRRRRRRR," in ecstasy. He squeezed her overpoweringly tight. "SSSSSSHHH,"

Jackson, she screamed as she stroked his cock faster and faster. He moaned, "Sit on my cock." She unzipped her pants and sat on his hard throbbing cock. OOOOOOOOOOHHHHHHHHHHHHHH, Jackson your cock feels GOOOOOOOOOOD. She straddled his cock; riding it faster and faster. She screamed, "AAAAAAHHHHHHHHH, Jackson, I'm cuming; I'm CUUUMMMIIIINNGGGG FOOOOOOOOOOOOOOHHHHHHHHH, Jackson." She came all over his balls. Shit Carmen! Your CUUMMMM is hot. OOOOOHHHHH, he moaned and groaned, "SSSSSSSHHHHHHHH, please make me CUUUUUUMMMMMMMMM. YEEEEEEEEEEEEEEESSSSSSSSSSSSSSSS, ride my cock. Shit Carmen! Ride my cock. I want you to make me CUUUUUUMMMMMMMMMMMM. Baby make to CUUUUUUUUUUUUUUM."

An announcement came over the Intercom – Flight 167 departing for Seattle, Washington is boarding. Shit Jack! The plane is boarding early. I know Baby but make me CUUUUUUUMMMM before you leave. YEEEEEEEEEES, make me CUUUUUUUUUUUUMMMMMMMMM. Shit, OOOOOOHHH, AAAAAAHHHHHH, I'm CUUUMMMIIIIINNNNGGGGGG.

Last call for Flight 167 departing for Seattle, Washington. Jackson, I don't want to miss my flight. They quickly stopped as they uncontrollably laughed while fixing their clothing. They arrived at the gate. "Baby, thank you for this wonderful weekend!" He kissed her holding her incredibly tight. I will call you later today to see if you arrived home safely. No Jack! I have a prior commitment with Jessie. "Are you planning to stay with him?" Jackson, that's none of your business. You are right. But, I will call anyway; if you are not home, I will leave a message. Okay Jack, have a super meeting! She turned waving good-bye to him. She blew him a kiss as he waved moving his mouth saying, "I will miss you!" She walked away – boarding the plane. She settled in her seat and closed her eyes thinking about her fun filled weekend. She felt embarrassed about her behavior; especially spending her weekend with a total stranger, but reflected back to the time she spent with him and thought, "He was a first-rate fuck." She sighed, "Perhaps, Jessie is even better."

Jack waited at the airport until Carmen's plane departed. He thought to himself as he walked to his car; this was the weekend of an entire lifetime. Gosh! I'm SOOOOOOOOO happy; I had an opportunity to meet her. I will miss her and can't wait until I see her in Washington. He moaned, "UUUUUUMMMMMMMM," I loved hearing her scream, "Jackson". He moaned, "AAAAAAAHH, Jackson. My name never sounded so sweet!"

Chapter Two

At Last

As Carmen walked through the airport in Seattle, she began smiling as she approached the shoeshine station. She reflected on, "Her experience with Jack at the Colorado Springs's airport." She squeezed her hands together, "If anyone had told me in advance, I would have such an outrageously wild weekend; I wouldn't have believed it." She gazed at her watch. Gosh! It's 5:00 A.M. "Only four hour before the boutique opens."

"Carmen Hailey is owner and operator of Boshae`. An upscale women-clothing boutique located downtown Seattle. The boutique's top designer fashions have captured the attention of numerous women from across the nation, and the "Private Fashion Shows" have captured the interest of numerous women – locally. Carmen's strong perseverance and commitment has developed her boutique into an exceptionally profitable business during the past six years."

She arrived home, quickly showered, and drove to the boutique. As she was leaving out the door for the boutique, she checked her messages. Beep! Hello Carmen, this is Jack. He corrected himself, "No! This is Jackson Harper; I had an amazing weekend with you. Thanks for the remarkable time! Baby, I never thought; I would have so much enjoyment in an airport – not in a million years. I can't stop thinking about your steamy hot, wet, cunt as I'm leaving this message." She cleared her throat. "Uh, cunt that's new. He didn't use cunt while we were together during the weekend." She shyly laughed. "Hell, Jackson is so full of surprises." He sounded so thrilled; I will call you tonight for an update on your rendezvous with Jessie and for some hot and steamy phone sex. She laughed at the top of your voice. "Jackson, I will not waste my time having phone sex with you; I'm not your horny wife." He said, "Oh by the way, you left your address book on the table in my room. Have an exceptional day at the boutique, and I will see you on Wednesday." She slammed the phone onto the receiver. Damn! Now, he knows my address. Oh well, I will tell Mr. Harper, "He's not welcome at my home or business whenever he chooses to visit."

She arrived at her boutique at 7:45 A.M., and Liz was already there. "Liz Carlson is Carmen's best friend. She has assisted Carmen at Boshae` during the past ten years. Although, the first three years of opening the boutique was definitely difficult to operate, they remained persistent in their efforts, and now, are extremely proud of their accomplishments." Liz walked over to Carmen, good morning, how was your weekend excursion? Carmen beamed with excitement! I had the time of my life. Next time, I will make plans to stay longer! Liz seemed as excited as Carmen. "So what did you do while you were there?" Lets see! I relaxed; meet some extraordinarily fascinating interesting people, and toured the city. "So did you meet anyone interesting?" She sighed, "I ran into several pleasantly nice men, but no one I was attracted to." Come on Carmen, I see that look in your eyes that you are not being truthful. She stated, "Liz, you are being awfully inquisitive." Liz placed her hands into her pockets. No! But, I know you didn't spend the entire weekend alone.

Last June when I flew to Jamaica, I met this man at the hotel restaurant. We knew we were attracted to each other and before an hour had passed we were fucking. Gosh Liz! I don't want to hear your personal business, but how big was his cock? Liz enthusiastically laughed. "I thought; you didn't want to hear my personal business. YEEEEEEEEES Carmen, his cock was gigantic; I have never fucked a cock that huge and girl was it GOOOOOOD. His cock was at least fourteen-inches long, and I took every bit of it." Carmen excitedly laughed. "You are over exaggerating; his cock wasn't really that huge." Liz raised her arms into the air. "Well, it might have been thirteen-inches." They both eagerly laughed. "You are too funny Liz." No! But, Carmen his cock was SOOOOOOOOOOOOOOOOOOOOOOOO GOOOOOOOOOOOOOOOOOOOOOOD.

I'm getting horny simply thinking about my trip to Jamaica. We spent the entire time together. Liz, do you still see him? Yes! We spent the past weekend together. Carmen placed her index finger into her mouth. Liz; I know that man isn't Lester Freeman! Yes Carmen! He's Lester Freemen. I always wondered how you met Lester. Carmen, that is how! Since, he lives out of town and, of course, married, I can only see him on frequent occasions. I'm surprise Carmen; you are not giving me the third degree for sleeping with an unavailable married man. Yes Liz! That's truly surprising, but you are grown, and you can fuck whomever you choose. Come on Carmen something happened this past weekend; you are not sharing with me. "Oh Liz, what make you believe that?"

First of all! You received two phone calls from Jackson Harper. "Did he leave any messages?" I told him; you had not arrived at the boutique. He said, "He would call you later." Also, look at those flowers on the counter. Carmen was flabbergasted, "They are beautiful! Where did they come from?" Liz glimpsed at the floor; I don't know. Come on Liz, now who isn't being truthful. Liz exhaled; "Well, I did sneak a quick peek, and they are from Jackson. He wanted to thank you for the lovely weekend. Now, these flowers imply to me; you showed Jackson an awesome time." Carmen interrupted Liz by clearing her throat, "We had dinner together." Liz inquired, "And, what else Carmen?" And, we sit out by the pool and talked for hours. Sure Carmen. Liz, you are behaving like my mother. No Carmen, but I don't believe you are telling the full truth! As she walked into her office, she said, "Liz, please change the subject and what's on the agenda for today?" Carmen, we have ten clients booked for today, so hopefully; the sales will bring great profits into Boshae`. "The past six weeks in sales have been remarkable!"

Carmen walked over to the counter to check the schedule to see who was booked. "Ring, ring, good morning Boshae`. Yes, she's here." Carmen, this call is for you. "Who is it?" It's Jackson. Liz asked, "Why such an enormous smile on your face Carmen?" Carmen softly laughed. "Liz, mind your business." Hello Jackson! I'm doing fine and you? "How was your business meeting?" Baby great! All pending issues were resolved today, so no more meetings are needed at this time. Marvelous Jackson, now, you can rest the remaining of the day. She sounded surprised, "You are what?" He answered, "I'm flying out this evening at 6:45 P.M." Fantastic Jackson, I'm sure Karen is really excited that you are coming home early; I thought you were staying until Wednesday. Yes! Those were my original plans, but I miss you a great deal, so I'm coming home to be with you. He asked, "Why are you whispering?" She eagerly laughed. "So my inquisitive assistance doesn't hear my conversation." He anxiously laughed. "Liz seems really nice." Jackson, she's my best friend but nosey as hell! Liz happily laughed. "Okay Carmen, I heard that." You see what I mean Jackson; it's unreal, but she hears everything. She asked so many questions especially when those flowers arrived at the boutique this morning. Thank you very much Jackson, but please don't send any more flowers and be extremely careful what you say in Liz's present. He cheerfully laughed. "Are you implying she has a big mouth?" Yes! Her mouth is as big as her ears. Okay Carmen, I heard that. "They both excitedly laughed."

No Jackson! I can't see you tonight; have you forgotten that I have plans with Jessie? He has made special plans for us tonight. I haven't seen Jessie in two weeks, so I look forward to seeing him. No Jackson! I'm not planning to stay at his home tonight, and no, I can't meet you later, but thanks for the invitation. He moaned, "UUUUUMM," I must go now, but I will call later tonight; if you are not there; I will call back later. Bye-Jackson. Bye-Baby, I will call tonight. Liz said, "I thought; you didn't fuck Jackson, but your face surely has an impression of being vigorously fucked." Carmen energetically laughed. "You are funnier than all get out!" "Now, how in the hell does a fuck face look? Liz touched Carmen's face, look into the mirror; you will see an energetic and laminating fuck face! They were laughing when Jessie Hopkins walked into the boutique. Carmen greeted him and asked, "What brings you here so early this morning? It's marvelous seeing you, Jessie, but I'm really surprise that you're here! I never expected to see you first thing this morning." He hugged her and said, "Beautiful flowers." Jessie, I met an incredibly kind gentleman while in Colorado Springs, and he was gracious enough to send thank-you flowers. "Oh, I helped him accomplished something for his wife. That's his way of showing gratitude." Jessie appeared baffled. He said, "Carmen; can I see the card?" Jessie, you are behaving as if you don't trust me. Sure, here's the card." He read the card, "Thanks for your help this past weekend, Jackson." She touched his arm, are you satisfied? It's only a token of appreciation. He handed her the card, so you are right; I'm sorry for second guessing you. He glimpsed into the ceiling. Carmen, things will change between us. I promise you. I have been alone for several years now, and I know

Pauline would like for me to go on with my life. After all, I will turn sixty-three in three months. She could clearly hear Jackson telling her, "Jessie is too old for you."

She leaned against the counter. "Hopefully, you will stop working so many late nights and began living your life to the fullest." Baby, I came to tell you; I'm retiring in two weeks. She blurted, "You are doing what Jessie?" Yes Baby! I'm retiring, so I can spend more time with you. I have kept you waiting long enough. She thought, "Shit what about my plan! I have dreams of expanding Boshae`; therefore, retirement doesn't fit into my plans anytime soon, and I'm happy that you are finally getting on with your life." He hugged her and said, "Baby you won't be disappointed with my decision; my plans are to make you the happiest woman in the world." Thinking to herself, "You are too late; Jackson has already done that!"

He squeezed her hands; can you have Liz operate the boutique while you and I drive to Vancouver to spend the day together? Jessie, do you really mean that? Please don't feel obligated to rush into anything. This is surely an extreme from last week of not having any time to creating too much time. He raised his voice; "Are you telling me you don't want to spend your life with me?" No Jessie! Please don't take what I'm about to say the wrong way, but even though you are retiring, I still have my business to operate. Boshae` is my livelihood. It keeps the roof over my head. Baby, I want to provide a livelihood for you. Jessie, please don't start demanding things from me at this critical time of my life. He asked, "Liz do you mind operating the boutique today while Carmen and I drive to Vancouver." No! I don't mind. "No, Jessie not now!" We have ten appointments, and Liz will not be able to assist everyone by herself. Sorry Carmen, I'm truly sorry! I realize you still have your business to operate and please forgive me if I appear to be insensitive. Our date is still plan for 6:00 P.M. I will send a driver here to pick you up. No Jessie! I must first drive home to shower and change clothing. Okay, I will send the driver to your home. Okay, thank you! He kissed her; I will see you later this evening. Bye. She smiled and said, "Bye."

Liz shook her head. Carmen, "What are you going to do with two men?" Last week, you didn't want to be involved with anyone, and this week you are involved with two men. Carmen, Jackson Harper is definitely not the man you want in your life. He is truly a "Forbidden Lover, and the both of you will be, "Caught in a web of lies, sex and deceit". Honey, you deserve more from a relationship, why not create a life with Jessie! Liz, "As if Jessie isn't a "Forbidden Lover." Liz, have you forgotten he and Shirley Wilson is dating? Carmen, he seems like an excellent catch.

Now Liz, you act as if I'm deep-sea fishing. "Don't be silly Carmen, this is only a figure of speech." Liz Sweetie, I know – I sometimes have terribly dry sense of humor.

You are so right Liz, "How does one woman manage her life with more than one man?" Carmen, it will not be easy; perhaps, loving two men will bring joy, tears, and plenty of drama. Carmen vigorously laughed. "I don't mind the drama." Liz gently laughed. "Yes! I know; you have always been an overly exaggerated drama queen." Carmen, don't slip and call Jackson by Jessie's name and Jessie by Jackson's name. Yea right. I sure hope not! "So Liz, what I do I call them?" Call them both; "Baby or Sweetie", that way you will never slip up; and you will always enjoy an exuberant fucking. Carmen passionately laughed. "You are so funny Liz but it does make a lot of sense." I know Carmen. I have slipped on many occasions so, "Baby" is always the best practice.

Mrs. Jenkins walked into the boutique. Darling, how are you this morning? I have two social events to attend this Friday, and I want something exquisitely beautiful to wear. I will browse around and if I assistant; I will yell for you or Liz. Carmen touched Liz's shoulder – please assist Mrs. Jenkins. As Liz talked with Mrs. Jenkins, Carmen began thinking about her weekend with Jackson. "UUUUUUUMMMMMMM, what an incredibly awesome weekend? Shit! I can never share this experience with anyone, not even my best friend, Liz." She began feeling extremely horny. Shit, not here at the boutique. She sighed. "I will accept Jessie's previous invitation. I really should stop avoiding him." Liz walked over. Carmen, I can see that look on your face again, "Why don't you leave?" Liz handed, Mrs. Jenkins several dresses and said, "Why don't you go into the fitting room and try them on?" While Mrs. Jenkins changed in the fitting room Liz said again, "Why don't you leave Carmen?" I will operate the boutique while; you are gone. She thanked Liz! I will make this up to you. Sweetie, I know you will.

Carmen, you have helped me on many occasions, so please leave and enjoy the day with Jessie. I will see you on Tuesday. Okay, thanks Liz! I will call him before I leave. Hello Jessie, this is Carmen, Is the invitation still open for the drive to Vancouver? Sure Baby! But, what changed your mind? Jessie, I couldn't stop thinking about you, and I really would like to know you much better. I'm going home, so I can pack; I will be at your home in forty-five minutes. Carmen couldn't figure out the sudden transformation in Jessie's behavior. She thought, "I truly don't believe; he's retiring from his job. His career has been his focus for many years. His job meant so much too him. I often thought with the long hours he worked; he would eventually pass away at his desk. Gosh! There is more to his decision than what he is telling me but over time the truth will surface."

As she entered her house the phone ranged. Hello. Hi Baby, Liz told me; you were on your way home. Hi Jackson. "Carmen, are you not feeling well today?" Yes Jackson! I'm feeling really terrific, but I'm taking the day off to spend with Jessie. "Why are you so quite Jackson?" I'm thinking Carmen. Jackson, "Thinking about what?" Carmen, you refused to stay an extra day in Colorado Springs with me because of your obligations to your boutique, but today you are taking time off to spend with Jessie. Yes! I am Jackson, but I have known Jessie for many years, and I want to spend time with him – something he and I haven't done since we met. "So what about us, Carmen?" I don't understand your question Jackson. Carmen, can we spend time together today? No Jackson! His voice became extremely harsh, was I only a good fuck to you this past weekend? No Jackson! But, I hope you don't expect for me to drop everything for you. No Carmen! I'm not asking you to drop everything for me, but please make time for us. "Didn't you enjoy spending the weekend with me?" Yes, I had a wonderful time Jackson, but all great things must come to an end! Jackson, your wife needs you more then anything in this world, so don't get involved in a situation that you will regret later. He shook his head. I know Karen needs me, but I'm certain; I can love the both of you. I don't believe so Jackson! I really want to make Jessie and my relationship gel. "If things don't work out Carmen than what? She sighed, "I will decide at that time." He whispered, "Carmen, can I see you on Wednesday?" Jackson, I don't know, please call me on Wednesday to check my schedule. "Can't we make plans now?" No Jackson! We can't make plans today for Wednesday. I must pack now. I told Jessie; I would be at his home within forty-five minutes. Okay Carmen! I will call on Wednesday. Okay, Bye-Jackson.

As Carmen drove to Jessie's home, she reminisced about her possible experience with him. She thought, "Gosh! Jessie doesn't seem romantic at all. He is always so serious. Nonetheless, I will have an open mind and hope for the best." Carmen ranged Jessie's doorbell. Hello Mr. Hopkins! Hello Ms. Hailey, I'm glad you were able to come! He extended his arms and hugged her extremely tight. I promise; you will not regret spending this day with me. She kissed him; I will hold you to your promise. He kissed her as she held him firmly in her arms. She thought, "What the hell, he may turn out to be remarkable?" He unbuttoned her blouse. Her heart was pounding against his chest. She was getting so excite until she thought she was losing control. OOOOOOHHHH shit Jessie! He placed his hands on her tits and caressed them rigidly. "UUUUUUMMMMMM, Jessie, your hands feel SOOOOOOOOO, damn, GOOOOOOOOOOD."

She pressed her lips firmly together as he sucked her nipples. AAAAAAAAAAHHHHHH, Jess. He whispered, "Come on Baby lets go upstairs. He took her by her hands and escorted her upstairs to his bedroom. I waited many years to embrace you in my arms, to make love to you as you desire." She moaned, "Jessie why did you wait SOOOOOOOOOO long? Damn! I wanted you for many years, but you were always in pursuit of climbing the corporate ladder." I'm sorry, Carmen; you have waited so long, but I didn't want to rush you into a relationship. She moaned, "SSSSSSSSSSHHHHHH, I can't wait to feel your cock stroking my pussey."

"AAAAAAAHHHHHH," he moaned, "I want to eat and fuck your pussey." She rested on the bed as he removed her pants. As he knelt in the bed, he beamed with excitement. His eyes were so mesmerizing. UUUUUUUMMMMMMM, his beard felt sensational rubbing against her tits. "OOOOOOOOOOOHHHHHHHHH, UUUUUUUUUUMMMMMMMMMMM," Jessie, I want you to lick my pussey. YEEEEEEEES, I want to feel your tongue licking my pussey. Jessie leaned over and slid his tongue down Carmen's stomach to her steamy pussey. He intensely kissed her pussey. Carmen was getting excited until she CUUUUUUUUUMMMMMMM even before his tongues touched her clit.

Oh, Baby your pussey is SOOOOOOOO sweet and wet. OOOOOOOHHHHHHHHH Carmen, your CUUUUUMMMMMMMMM is SOOOOOOOOOOOOOO sweet. He moaned, "Carmen, I want to fuck you." He removed his clothing, and his cock appeared to be at least fifteen-inches long. JEEEEEESSSSSSSSSSSSSSSSIE, your cock is SOOOOOOOOOOOOOOOOOOOO; he kissed her. He moaned, "SSSSSSSHHHHHH," as he slowly slid his cock into her pussey, "AAAAAAHHHHHHHHHHH." Shit Carmen your pussey is GOOOOOOOOOOOOD. She moaned and groaned, "UUUUUUMMMMMM, as she moved her ass back and forth on the bed faster and faster."

He was breathing out of control as sweat rolled down his forehead onto her face. Carmen, I had imagined your pussey would feel this great. Shit! Your pussey is better than I could have ever imagined. "AAAAAAAAHHHHHHHHHHH," Carmen, OOOOOHHHHHH. She thought, "For sixty-two years old, he certainly is an awesome fuck." OOOOOOOHHHHHHHHH Carmen, I'm CUUUUUUUUUMMMMMMMIIIINNNN NIIIIGGGG. OOOOOOOOHHHHHH, shit

Baby! I'm YEEEEEEEEEEEEEEEEEEEES! I'm CUUUUUMMMMMIIIIIINNNGGGGG!

He moaned and groaned, "AAAAHHH, thanks, your pussey felt GOOOOOOOOOOOD." He held her in his arms and said, "Lets rest before driving to Vancouver. Carmen, we will not stop seeing each other." Oh Jessie, lets not get carried away. They both willingly laughed. I'm serious Carmen. He awakened her whispering; "Lets get dress; it is getting late. We should leave shortly to beat the rush hour traffic." As he drove, she said, "I hope you don't mind, but I would like to nap while you drive. I'm awfully tired. She was extremely exhausted, since she stayed up all night." Sure Baby! Sleep as much as you like. He played Jazz music while he drove. She whispered, "UUUUUUUUUMMMMMMMMM. Jessie, the music is really relaxing." He agreed, "Yes! Jazz music is one of life's pleasures."

She asked, "So where are we staying Jessie." At Keystone Cottage Inn, there is one also located in Colorado Springs. She slightly smiled. "What was the importance of telling me that a Keystone Inn is located in Colorado Springs?" He squeezed her hand, no particular reason! But I'm sure you will like it. It's extremely cozy. She held his hand; I'm quite sure I will like it. He cleared his throat; over the past few years, I have contemplated operating a Bed and Breakfast. She seemed overly excited, Jessie, that's an extraordinary idea! If you don't follow through, perhaps that will be one of my long-term goals. She inquired, "Have you stayed at the Keystone Inn before?" Yes! I have Carmen. She moaned, "UUUUUMMMMMM," with Pauline or Shirley? With Pauline, but of course, that was many years ago. Jessie, please don't tell me about the things you and Pauline experienced while staying there. "Lets create our own memories." Carmen, that's what I had in mind. She sighed, "Thanks Jessie." He drove around town stopping at various shops, and gardens. "There is so much to do and see here in Vancouver but, "AAAAAHHHHH," we are slightly limited to how we spend our evening." As he drove over to the Cottage Inn, he whispered, "Why don't we make reservation tonight when we check-in to return for an entire week?" She kissed his cheek. Gosh Jessie! I really don't know; I must check my schedule before committing to being away for an entire week. He squeezed her hand; Carmen, please don't get so preoccupied with your business that you forget there is an exciting world awaiting to embrace you. Yes Jessie! I have been warned on numerous occasions!

He touched her arm; I know of an extraordinarily quaint restaurant; it's fairly small but awfully cozy. As they ate dinner, they talked and laughed. Jessie, do you regret being sixty-two and now realizing there's much in life you should have experienced while spending countless hours at your office. No Baby! Because, I enjoyed everything, I have experienced and accomplished in my life! Yes! I worked many long hours and didn't spend as much time at home with Pauline as I should have, but I have truly enjoyed my past. He sighed, "If I had spent many years working and didn't get any fulfillment, then my job would have been in vain." Yes Jessie! I know what you mean! I have worked many years creating Boshae` into an extremely successful business, and I have truly enjoyed my efforts during the process. Yes! I know there's a grandiose life awaiting to embrace me, but there is so much I want to accomplish at Boshae` and not many years left. Once, I have achieved my goals; I will pull away from my business and have someone else operate it. But first! "I must establish the fundamentals of a rock-solid business foundation before my retirement plans could ever come into fruition. Jessie, you were not pressured into retiring, and I would like the same freedom to decide when to retire, but not until I'm at peace with my business accomplishments. Liz is great with the day-to-day operation of Boshae`, and perhaps, she will agree to continue operating our business. If not, she and I will hire someone to manage the boutique for us."

He paid the check; are you ready to leave? Sure! But, I must call Liz at home to see how things went today. "Can't you discuss your business affairs with

Liz on tomorrow." Yes Jessie, I can! But, I prefer calling her tonight. Sure Baby! It appears; you and Liz have established an inseparable strong business partnership. Yes! Liz and I have been business partners for many years not too mention best friends. We are like sister. She has been my assistant, since I opened Boshae`, ten years ago. Liz and I have morally supported each other through many circumstances.

When she got into the car, she called Liz. Hello Liz, it's Carmen. I'm calling to see how things went today. Liz appeared exceedingly energized. Carmen, "The clients blew the roof off the boutique with their purchases. Mrs. Smith purchased a remarkably chic new wardrobe for her niece who recently graduated from college. She wants her niece to make an exceptionally great impression in her new career. Ms. Lincoln is a new client." Great Liz! We always want new clients. Liz continued talking, "Ms. Lincoln located to Seattle from Chicago and heard about the boutique from Mrs. Jenkins during last Friday's social event. She's in broadcasting which means she must always look her best. Hopefully! She will inform her colleagues about Boshae`. Ms. Lincoln was really indecisive; nonetheless, she purchased the cream of the merchandise, and she has impeccable taste in her wardrobe. Gosh, her purchase was substantially large!"

Liz sympathetically laughed. "Mrs. Taylor and Mrs. McGee were here shopping together, and it almost appeared; they were competing too see who could purchase the most expensive items. Unfortunately, there were four cancellations, but the sales for today sufficed the cancellations." Thanks Liz! The sales were off the hook and your sales performance was outstanding. How many clients are scheduled for Tuesday? Carmen, "We have eight appointments on Tuesday." Great Liz! But, I will be in late on Tuesday. Liz sounded extremely compassionate. Carmen take as much time as you need; you really deserve this time away from the boutique. I will guard the fort down until you return. "Have an enjoyable time with Jessie, and I will see you on Tuesday evening. Oh, Jackson called as soon as you left." I know Liz; he called when I arrived home. Liz have a great evening, and Sweetie, you will be compensated for your time! Bye-Girlie. Bye-Liz.

While Jessie drove, she rested her head on his shoulder. She placed her arms around and said, "You can have me to yourself the rest of the night." They checked into the Keystone Inn. As they talked, echoes sounded the door. He opened the door to the delivery of champagne. She smiled. Jessie, this is really lovable of you! Approximately, five minutes later another knock came at the door. He opened the door, and there were many red and yellow long stem roses delivered to her.

She hugged him and said, "Jessie, you are full of surprises tonight. Thanks so much!" He cleared his throat. "I didn't want Jackson out performing me." He called me this morning. Carmen sat in the chair, "Why the hell did Jackson call you; I really don't believe, he had the nerves to call you." He warned me to stop playing games with you. She replied, "So is that the main reason for us being here tonight?" No Carmen! Jackson made me realized that I'm wasting your time. He told me; you are an amazingly awesome person, and I should stop wasting your time. He questioned, "Why in the hell should you have to fly to Colorado Springs for excitement!" I'm sorry Jessie that Jackson took it upon himself to call you. Tears rolled from her eyes. "I used his phone last night to call you and accidentally left my address book on the table in his hotel room. But that didn't give him the right to go through my address book calling whomever he desired."

Jessie became furious, "Why the hell were you in his room last night and how did you meet him?" He raised his arms over his head, "How much of me did you discuss with Jackson?" She stood from the chair, "We didn't discuss you to a great extent, but I did tell Jackson upon Pauline passing away you buried yourself in your work." Shit Carmen! "How could you discuss my personal business with a total stranger and not with me?" Hell Jessie, I tried discussing this issue with you, but you were always so full of bullshit, until I became frustrated hearing the same excuses over and over. He walked closer to her, so did you fuck him? "Why are you asking me this question, Jessie? He angrily stared at her. "Did you fuck him?" She slightly rested against the table. She sighed, "What did Jackson tell you?" Carmen, he was as evasive as you are being at the moment. Damn Jackson! Your question is irrelevant. He yelled, "Like hell – it's irrelevant." "What if I told you; I slept with Jackson – than what? Will you tell me; you don't want to see me any more? What about you and Shirley Wilson?" Carmen, how dare you bring up her name? She raised her voice, "How dare you ask me if I fucked Jackson Harper this past weekend? How long have you been fucking Shirley?" He sighed, "What are we doing, Carmen?" We didn't drive this distant to argue with each other. "Yes! I have fucked Shirley on numerous occasions, but now I realized you are the only lady; I desire in my life." She maliciously said, "After you realized, I will not sit idle and wait for you. Yes Jessie! I fucked Jackson. I fucked him all night long. Now are you satisfied with my answer? If you believe, I have plans to continue waiting on you; you are sadly mistaken." She walked over to the bed. "I'm tired; Jessie. Goodnight. I will talk with you when I awaken in the morning."

He pressed his hand against his forehead; I want to massage your body. It will help you sleep much better. He began massaging her back extremely rough. His hands felt like magic. He whispered, "Did Jackson massage your body?" She sat up in bed, Jessie; I have heard enough of your nonsense. Please don't discuss Jackson any more tonight unless you willing to discuss "SW." He asked, "SW." She smiled. "Don't you know her initials? – Shirley Wilson." Jessie continued massaging her back. "AAAAAHHHH." He rolled her over onto her back and said, "Baby, do you feel like fucking all night." Sure Jessie, but do you have the vitality to fuck all night? He seemed stunned by her response. Gosh Jessie, I apologize – that was extremely insensitive of me to say that to you. He sighed, "I shouldn't be getting angry with you for seeing someone else. I really can't expect for you to wait forever." Hell, "Don't fool yourself Jessie; Jackson isn't the only one. He's the only one foolish enough to call you". He caressed and kissed her tit.

OOOOOOHHHH, I want to fuck your pussey, YEEEEEEESSSSSSSSSSSSSS. As he passionately slid his cock back and forth in her steamy hot pussey, he moaned, "OOOOOHHHHH, what do you mean Jackson isn't the only one." She whispered, "Would you stop talking about Jackson and fuck me?" Lets not waste an extremely GOOOOOOOOOOOOOOOOD fuck over insignificant issues. She moaned and groaned, "SSSSSSSSSSSSSSSSSHHHHHHHHHH, UUUUUUUUUUMMMMMMMMMMMM, you are excellent. Don't stop fucking me Jessie;" but he stopped. He firmly slid his tongue back and forth on her clit as she moved her ass back and forth on the bed whispering, "OOOOOOOOOHHHHHHHHH, JEEEEEEEESSSSSSSSSSSSSSSIIIIIIIIIIEEEEEEEE, your tongue is so HOOOOOOTTTTTT and it feels SOOOOOOOOOOOOOOOOOOOOOOO GOOOOOOOOOOOOOOOOOOOOOOD. UUUUUUUUUUMMMMMMMMMMMMM. Fuck my pussey. YEEEEEEEESSSSSSS, Jessie, I'm CUUUUUMMIIIIIIIIIIINNNNNNNNGGG." She was sweating and her pussey wanted more of his cock. I want your cock caressing my pussey. He moaned, "EEERRRRRRRRRRRRRRRRRR, I want to fuck you all night long. YEEEEEEEESSSSS, Baby, fuck me, fuck me, fuck my pussey." YEEEEEEEEEESSSSSSS, he moaned as he moved his cock faster and faster into her hot steamy pussey. His body was dripping sweat all over her body. She caressed his back as she kissed his shoulders. She moaned, "AAAAAAAAAHHHHHHH," as she asked for more and more of his stiff cock. "UUUUUUUMMMMM, Jessie deeper, deeper – Baby fuck, my pussey deeper." YEEEEEEEESSSS Baby, I will fuck you as deep as you like. Shit Carmen!

Your pussey is hot. "AAAAAAAHHHHH. Carmen, I'm CUUUUMMIIIIINNNGGGG." No, Jessie don't stop! "I'm CUUUUMMMIIIIIINNNGGGGG. SSSSSSSSSSSSSSSHHHHHHHHHH, UUUUUUUUUUMMMMMMMMMMM, YEEEEEEEEEESSSSSSSSSSSSSSSSS, it felt SOOOOOOO damn GOOOOOOOOOD." He rested his body against the bed as she rested her head on his chest. He caressed her shoulders and whispered, "How old is Jessie?" She didn't respond. He squeezed her arm please answer me. Gosh Jessie! Don't you ever give up? Jackson is fifty-six. Please don't ask anything else concerning him because I'm not discussing him anymore tonight. So please stop with your one million questions. Carmen, "What if I referred to your friend as "J"? She shook her head, "Jessie, you're not amusing at all! "Didn't, you call Shirley Wilson "SW"? Sure, I did! But, you will not get away with calling Jackson "J". I'm awfully tired Jessie; I would like to rest. He responded, "Are you implying Jackson and I have exhausted you?" She responded, "Jackson more so than you." He angrily laughed and wrapped his leg around her body extremely tight. "Carmen, you really know how to cause pain." She whispered, "You caused this pain on yourself, Jackson." He continued squeezing her body tightly with his leg, "What did you call me Carmen?" Sorry

Jessie, but I have heard enough of Jackson's name for one night. Goodnight Carmen! Goodnight Jessie. She rolled over in bed and fell asleep.

Jessie eating her pussey awakened her. "OOOOOOHHHHHHHHHHHHHHHHH, Jessie, UUUUUUUUUMMMMMMMM. This is an astonishingly way to be awakened each morning." He moaned, "AAAAAAHHHHHHHH, I can't get enough of you. I want to fuck you again and again and never stop." Thinking to herself, "That's the same thing Jackson told me." As she thought about Jackson, she became so aroused. "AAAAAAHHH," Jessie. He slid his finger back and forth into her pussey as he caressed her clit with his tongue. "SSSSSSSSSSSSHHHHHHHHHHHHHHH, Jessie, UUUUUNNNNNNNNNNN." She moved her ass back and forth moaning and groaning, "AAAAAAAAAAHHHHHHHHHHHHHH, AAAAAAAAAAAAAAHHHHHHHHHH," as his finger moved faster and faster in her pussey. YEEEEEEEEESSSSSSSSSSS please don't stop. YEEEEEEEEEEEEEESSSSSSSSSSSSSSSSS, "Ja," she caught herself as she almost screamed, "Jackson's name." YEEEEEEEESSSSSSSSSSSSS, Sweetie, she came over his finger and his tongue. He leaned over and kissed her pussey and said, "Gosh! It's Tuesday morning." She ran her hand through his beard. Yes, it is! And, I must get back to manage my boutique.

He kissed her shoulder; it would be nice if we could stay one more day. No! I really should get back today. Come on Carmen! Liz really gets pleasure from operating the boutique during your absence. I know she does, but I never wish to take her for granted. She thought; "Jackson is flying home tonight. It would be nice spending time with him, but this will only create dishonesty within our lives. Jackson will begin lying to Karen, and I will likewise with Jessie. Shit, we will eventually get caught in our lies!" She sat on the side of the bed; Jessie if you would like – please call me on Wednesday night.

He caressed her back; lets take shower together. No Jessie! I really must arrive at the boutique before noon, and it's already 8:45 A.M. He kissed her back, go ahead and shower first. She returned from the bathroom wearing a red short dress. He exhaled noisily, "Are you wearing that dress to the boutique today?" Sure Jessie! Is it too red or too short! He didn't answer. She walked over to the bed; please get up and shower, so we can drive back to Seattle. Sure Baby! Give me ten minutes. While walking to the car, he asked, "Would you like to stop for breakfast?" Yes Jessie! Breakfast sounds good but lets pickup something to eat while we are driving. While driving, he proposed, "Lets continue our relationship; where we are now!" Sure Jessie. But, we shouldn't rush anything!

She exhaled; it's still hard to believe; you are planning to retire. Carmen, I'm not getting younger, and it's time for me to enjoy the pleasures of life. I have worked all my life trying to acquire the finer things in life, but there is something still missing. I need an astonishing woman, and I know; she's you. Gosh Jessie! You really don't mean that. Sure, I do Carmen! It has taken years for me to realize this, and I know; we have missed out on creating many precious memories together. We can never regained the time we've lost, but we can treasure the time we have now. Tell me Jessie, how did you arrive at this revelation. He became extremely quite. She touched his arm. "Why are you so quite Jessie? I know you didn't make this decision based upon your conversation with Jackson."

You know Carmen, I'm glad he called. At first! I was angry with that son of a bitch but after being quite and listening to what the man had to say. I realized; everything he said was absolutely true. You are special and yes, you are full of fire not to mention an excellent fuck. But seriously Carmen, I've had feelings for you for a long time but my career always came first. He moaned, "Do you remember when we first met, and I asked you to spend the weekend with me. After you rejected me, I was crusted because; "No" woman had ever rejected me." She turned in her seat looking at him and jokingly said, "Were your ego crushed. Jessie you were married when I first met you. My strong morality wouldn't allow me to get involve with a married man, but hell things have drastically changed in my life." He caressed her legs. She sighed, "After Pauline passed away, you had gotten involved with Shirley, and I knew she was great emotional support for you, so I walked away." Jessie, various situations within our personal lives – influences us to take directional paths that we know are totally unethical. Although, we know what we're doing is totally wrong, we continue all for a moment of what we believe is true happiness. I know; I will eventually hate the lifestyle I have created, but I will deal with the problems as they occur.

She laid her head against the seat as she talked with him, how is Shirley doing these days? Carmen, she is doing great! But, I have never been really interested in Shirley! Carmen sighed, "So, how did you meet her?" Pauline introduced Shirley and I years ago. She thought Shirley would be an excellent wife for me once she passed on. Carmen at first! I thought Shirley was my soul mate, but damn; I could never stop thinking about you! "I continued seeing Shirley because I didn't want to disappoint, Pauline, but hell Carmen; Pauline is no longer with me, and I'm still trying to please her as I did while she was living." He ran his hand through his beard, I can't continue living my life this way. My life is missing zest. If there is such a thing, "Pauline and I shall see each other again during the after life – we will discuss it at that time, but for now I'm living my life to its fullest." And hopefully Carmen, it's with you. She exhaled, "Have you discussed this issue with Shirley?" No! But, I'm planning to have this same talk with her. "So Jessie, what are you waiting on? Don't, tell me that you are deceiving, Shirley."

He sped up the car, "Come on Carmen don't be difficult." No Jessie! I'm not being difficult, but Shirley has feelings, and she has a right to know where she stands with you. She placed her arm around his neck. Were Pauline and Shirley good friends? Yes! They grew up together, best friends since four years old. Pauline and I traveled frequently with Shirley and her husband. Robert passed away six years ago from a heart attack and Shirley never remarried. She continued traveling with Pauline and me. Once Pauline was diagnosed with cancer, she wanted me to remarry, but with Shirley. I agreed at that time because I thought Pauline's idea was great. He moaned, "AAAAAAAAHHHHH, Shirley and Robert married straight out of high school." They both worked and attended college. They never had children, so they always spent time with Pauline and me, "Probably for the reason that we also didn't have children either." The four of us had so much in common but after getting to know Shirley on an extremely personal level; "I realized she and I had nothing in common, at all." Jessie, I know over the years; you have made love to Shirley on numerous occasions. Yes! I have Carmen. "And". "And what, Carmen?" Nothing Jessie, I would like to change the subject. He drove into the parking lot. She thanked him for driving her back safely to her boutique in one piece. She kissed his cheek and said, "For one moment; I thought you would be stopped for speeding." She hugged him. "Thanks for the open and honest conversation. Hopefully, we will have similar conversations in the future."

He smiled. You can count on that. He also thanked her for the lovely evening. He leaned over and kissed her. He moaned, "UUUUUUMMMM," is it okay to call you later?" As she glanced away, she noticed Jackson peeking from her boutique's window. She became slightly excited; she kissed Jessie and whispered, "Why don't you spend time with Shirley tonight? I know she is worried that she didn't hear from you last night." Gosh Carmen! I would love to spend tonight with you but if you insist. I will call Shirley. "Yes Jessie, I insist!" Bye-Baby, thanks for everything. Bye-Jessie.

Chapter Three

The "Private Show"

Carmen stood outside the boutique until Jessie drove away. She opened the door and was greeted by Jackson's smile. She frowned. "What are you doing here Jackson?" Carmen, a hello would be sufficient! Hello Jackson, "Now what are you doing here?" He smiled. "I stopped by to say, hello." She walked into her office, and then asked, "Do you have my address book?" He gave her the address book. She blurted; "I don't believe you called Jessie. I'm competent enough to take care of myself; therefore, I don't want you calling my friends giving them your opinions on how I should be treated!" He cleared his throat; "My phone call made an enormous change in Jessie's behavior? It suddenly became urgent for him to spend time with you?" She sat in her chair, Jackson; those plans were already made prior to me flying home from Colorado Springs. Should you be given credit for Jessie's plan? Now Jackson, whom the hell else have you called? He sat on her desk and folded his arms; I thought Jessie should know the truth. She yelled, "Jackson, the truth about what?" He calmly asked, "Why are you so angry?" Carmen, Jessie was clueless about your feelings toward him. He did admit spending long hours at the office. Jackson placed his hand underneath his chin, "Carmen; now he knows how you feel and if he isn't interested, he can move on with his life, and you can do likewise." Shit Carmen! Why aren't you appreciative that I'm looking out for your best interest? She stood from her chair, what the hell do you know about protecting my, "My best interest." I believe you should first look after your wife's best interest. She needs you more than I will ever need you.

She sat on the desk beside him, so how was your night when you arrived home last night? "AAAAAAAAAAAHHHHHHHHHH," it was the best. Karen and I fucked all night. Jackson, you are simply an energized fucking machine. He said, "Speaking of fucking machine, what about a quick fuck now?" No Jackson! I'm at work. He touched her arm, your office seems like an excellent spot too me. She stood from sitting on the desk. No! I have an appointment in one hour. He lightly smiled. I would love to hear about your rendezvous with Jessie? She stared out the window; the time spent with Jessie was outstanding. We both felt this time together was long overdue or should I say, "At Last". He walked over and stood behind her, so how was Jessie? She turned and glimpsed into his eyes, Jackson; "What kind of question is that?" He shrugged his shoulders, only a routine question. Well, Jessie and I talked candidly about his personal life. Also, we discussed Shirley Wilson. He expressively asked, " Who is Shirley Wilson?" Carmen closed her eyes; Shirley is Pauline's best friend. Pauline wanted Jessie to marry Shirley, once she passed away. He touched the plant leaf, "So, how did Jessie manage to spend the night away from Shirley?" She didn't answer.

She walked over to her desk. Jackson, I have my business to operate; therefore, I really need for you to leave. He moaned, "AAAAAAAAHHHHHH, you look sexy in this red dress. Did you know red is my favorite color?" She shook her head, "No Jackson! I didn't know." He glanced at his watch, can, I take you out for lunch? No Jackson! I have several appointments; so I can't leave. He walked over to her, what about Liz operating the boutique until you return? Come on Jackson, Liz, isn't totally responsible for the success of Boshae`. He softly whispered, "I really like Liz." She shrugged her shoulders. He smiled, "I believe in due time, Liz and I will become great friends." Meaning what Jackson? He shrugged his shoulders. Exactly, what I said earlier, "Liz and I will become great friends." He tried hugging her. She backed away. "No Jackson, not now!" He kissed her lips, come on Carmen – hug me. Why are you being such a prude? She smirked, "Jackson, I'm not being a prude, but Mrs. Jenkins will be arriving in thirty minutes or less." He ran his hand through her hair; is she as sizzling as you? Carmen, please answer me? He kissed her; I will stick around to find out for myself. She pulled away from him. "No Jackson! You are not staying here to interfere with my clientele." Oh, lighten up Carmen, I'm only teasing!

He whispered, "I can see that look in your eyes." She whispered, "What look Jackson?" I can sense Carmen; you want me to eat your pussey while you lie on your desk. Jackson, I wasn't thinking that, but it sounds extremely alluring. He moaned in her ear, "UUUUUUUUUUUUUMMMMMMMMMMMM, my cock is getting so hard barely looking at you." He kissed her forehead; I will make it quick before Mrs. Jenkins arrive for her appointment. No Jackson, Liz is here! Shit Carmen! Kiss me. I promise; I not to turn you on! Too late Jackson! I'm already turned on. "SSSSSSSSSHHHHHHHHHHHHHH," Baby, kiss me. No Jackson, the door is opened! He walked over and shut the door and dimmed the lights. He took her by the hand, leading her to the desk. She gleefully sat down and rested her back against the desk. She lifted her ass while he removed her nylon. He moaned, "UUUUUUUUUUUUUMMMMMMMMMMMM; I love these red thongs." He slowly knelt in front of her as he energetically caressed his tongue over her thigh until he reached her pussey. She moaned, "AAAAAAAAAHHHHHHHHHHHHHHH, SSSSSSSSSSSSSSSSSSHHHHHHHHHHHH, AAAAAAAAAAAAAAAHHHHHHHHHH." He caressed his tongue back and forth over her clit while she slid her ass back and forth against her desk. 'AAAAAAAAAAAAAAAAAHHHHHHHHH, UUUUUUUUUUUUMMMMMMMMMMM," she was getting louder. Liz knocked on the door. "Carmen is everything okay?" Yes Liz, everything is okay! Liz repeated, "Are you sure?" Jackson yelled, "Everything is okay, Liz. Thanks for asking." Carmen glanced at her watch. Shit Jackson! You really must leave. She stood from her desk; I have an appointment with Mrs. Jenkins's. He seemed annoyed, can't Mrs. Jenkins wait. No Jackson! Mrs. Jenkins can't wait! She pays Liz's and my salary. He anxiously asked, "Will you come over tonight and give Karen a "Private Show" on your new fall wardrobe." No Jackson! I'm not participating in a threesome with Karen and you tonight! He irritably responded, "Who said anything about participating in a threesome, I'm asking for a "Private Show" for my wife tonight." Right Jackson, you are truly concern about your wife's Fall Wardrobe. Come on Carmen, "Why are you being so difficult?" Okay Jackson, I will give Karen a "Private Show" and that's it. I'm not fucking the two of you! Fine Carmen, I'm not asking you too. She sighed, "What time should I arrive?" He moaned, "SSSSSSSSHHHHHH, AAAHHHHHHHHHH, 6:30 P.M is a great time!" She sat at her desk, "What are Karen's favorite colors and most importantly, I need her garment and shoe sizes. Jackson, I will also need your street address." He rubbed his chin. Well let's see Carmen, "Karen, favorite colors are reds, purples, greens, and browns. She wears a size ten." He ran his hand through his hair; "I'm unsure of her shoe size." He gave her the address. She muttered, Jackson; it's probably best to bring Karen here at 6:30 P.M. I will have more selections for her to choose from. Carmen, I know Karen will feel extremely special if you came to the house for the "Private Show." Her eyes gleamed. I will see you at 6:30 P.M. As he left her office, he said, "Please wear something sexy." Bye-Jackson.

Liz walked into Carmen's office and said, "I know; you didn't fuck him here in your office." Now, Liz whatever do you mean! Jackson and I were discussing business issues. He's a savvy businessman, and I believe; I can learn a lot from him. Liz smiled. "I sense, Jackson is exceedingly smart, and he's also extremely sexy!" Carmen cheerfully laughed and gently pinched Liz's arm. "Keep your raging hormones away from him." They both forcefully laughed. You bet Carmen! Lester is more than enough for me.

Carmen was talking out aloud, "What should I take to at the Harpers' tonight?" Liz appeared extremely surprised, "Carmen, am I hearing you correctly?" Yes Liz! Jackson invited me over tonight at his home to give his wife a "Private Show." Liz shook her head; don't tell me you are planning to accept his invitation? Carmen walked out into the boutique; you bet I am! I know; Jackson will spend the money even if he didn't like the outfits. She began looking through the racks; I want to select items that will look remarkably stunning on Karen. "Jackson will not believe his eyes upon seeing Karen's transformation into an inspiring beauty queen."

Carmen declared, "Liz, you have a gift for selecting clothing that attract others, and so will you please help me prepare for the "Private Show." Sure Carmen, "This will be my pleasure! What are Karen's favorite colors and styles?" Oh Liz, please select clothing and accessories in reds, purples, greens, and browns. Oh in a size ten, but I'm unsure of her shoe sizes. Whatever styles you assume she will like! Please work your magic for me tonight – with about fifteen outfits. Hopefully Liz, Karen will like everything! Liz assured Carmen that Karen and Jackson would be pleased with everything – so please don't worry. It has happened in the pass, so tonight won't be any differently. Carmen glanced at the clock; oh Liz, Mrs. Jenkins and her husband will be here within five minutes. You know she is always on time. She wants her husband to see her in the red dress; she tried on yesterday. She wasn't sure whether he would like it. Liz please prepare for this evening, and I will help the Jenkins.

The boutique door opened, oh, Mrs. Jenkins you are here on time as usual. I was expecting you right about now. Mrs. Jenkins teased, "Can you squeeze me in now?" Carmen teasingly said, "No Mrs. Jenkins, since you have a bad habit of being late, you must wait! Okay Mrs. Jenkins, I will squeeze you in this time, but in the future you must wait." "Mr. and Mrs. Jenkins both happily laughed." Yes Darling, I will be on time in the future! Darling, this is Mr. Jenkins. Carmen extended her hand; it's a pleasure meeting you, Mr. Jenkins. Carmen, please call me Randolph. Randolph, it's a pleasure meeting you. Mrs. Jenkins, I understand you are here to model the red dress for Randolph. That's right Darling! Carmen said, "I was told that you look absolutely stunning wearing that dress." Why thank you Darling, I hope Randolph thinks so! I'm sure he will like how sexy you look in the dress! Randolph lightheartedly said, "Well Ruth, if you look as sexy as Carmen, I will buy you ten of those red dresses." Carmen replied, "She will look stunning and sexy, and so Randolph I will ring them up immediately." The three of them vigorously laughed. Carmen handed the red dress to Mrs. Jenkins; you know where the fitting room is located. Sure Darling, I will be out in a jiffy!

Carmen talked casually to Randolph as they waited for Ruth to return from the fitting room. He passionately licked his lips; you look lovely in red. Carmen, jokingly said, "Thanks RANDOLPHHH." Liz walked from the office looking at Carmen with a smirk on her face as if to say, "Carmen what are you up to." Liz returned to the office thinking, gosh, Jackson cologne smells awesome; I must find out what he is wearing!

Randolph reached into his coat pocket and handed Carmen his business card; please call me next week. I would love to take you to dinner. She inquired; "Will Mrs. Jenkins be joining us?" He cleared his throat. "No, to be honest, I really would love to spend time with you – getting too know you better." She didn't respond. He touched her arm; are you surprised Carmen? She confidently said, "No not at all." Mrs. Jenkins walked from fitting room, Randolph, how do I look? He said, "WOW, you look as stunning as Carmen said you would!" Randolph, does that mean Carmen can pack ten dresses for me? Ruth Baby, whatever you like! When she returned into the fitting room; he joke, "I will buy ten dresses only if you are willing to fuck me, Carmen." Randolph, I'm not willing. He slightly smiled. I knew that; I enjoy joking as much as Ruth. Carmen shook her head, "Were you really joking Randolph especially, since, your cock is bulging in your pants?" He walked closer to her; I feel like fucking you right now while Ruth watch or join in on the fun. She was disgusted with him and said, "What is it with men wanting to participate in threesomes?" "UUUUUUUUMMMMMMMM," Carmen, it's a quest to fulfill a deep and dark fantasy. She responded, "Don't expect for me to fulfill your fantasy!" He smirked.

Mrs. Jenkins returned from the fitting room handing the dress to Carmen. Carmen thanked her; will this be all Mrs. Jenkins? I received several shipments of fur coats and shoes that will go perfect with your dress. Have a seat, while I go into the back to get your shoes. Ruth joyful smiled as Randolph kissed her cheek. When Carmen returned with the shoes, he was caressing Ruth's legs. As she walked closer, she noticed, Randolph placing Ruth's hand on his stiff cock. Ruth had a big smile on her face. He kissed her lips vigorously! Carmen handed Ruth the shoes. Ruth tried the shoes and said, "Yes Darling, these shoes are perfect with my dress! YEEEEESSSSS Darling, I will purchase these shoes." Carmen smiled. "So, what is the big occasion?" Randolph divulged, "Ruth's best friend is getting married for the sixth time, and everyone is acting as if this is a blessed event." Carmen laughed and rung up the sale. She walked the Jenkins to the door, "Have fun at the wedding." Randolph turned and whispered, "Please call me."

Liz walked over too Carmen; I couldn't help but notice your behavior with Mr. Jenkins. Oh, Liz. I was only joking with Randolph. She hugged Liz; I'm leaving now to make sure I arrive at the Harpers' home by 6:30 P.M. Liz, I didn't get Karen's shoe size. Carmen, mission accomplished. I called Karen and told her; we have several new shipments of shoes and wanted to hold her a few pairs. Carmen raised her hands in the air, damn Liz; you are remarkable! I don't know what I would do without your assistance. Liz sarcastically said, "It would be awfully hard for you to manage this boutique without me." Carmen smiled. "I will see you on Wednesday." Carmen, please don't do anything that you will regret later." As she walked out the door, Liz said, "Have fun but not too much fun." Bye-Liz, have a goodnight with Melvin. As Liz walked away she said, "Lester is in town until Friday." Carmen gently laughed. "I thought you were acting awfully excited today. I even detected an illuminating fuck face." Liz quickly said, "You should know what an illuminating fuck face look like, since you've had one for the pass several weeks."

Carmen rushed home showered and dressed. She fiercely rummaged through her closet trying to find something sexy to wear to the Harpers' home. She dressed in a red skirt with a red and black printed blouse. Hell no! I don't like this outfit. She decided to wear her red leather miniskirt and a silk black low cut sleeveless blouse with a pair of red pumps. "UUUUUMMMM," I will wear my crouchless panties and stockings with a garter belt. She gave the impression of being extremely delighted with her reflections in the mirror. "This is perfect!"

She arrived at the Harpers' home right at 6:30 P.M. She ranged the doorbell. Jackson opened the door, "UUUUUUUMMMMM;" I won't be able to keep my eyes off of you tonight? Come in. She thanked him. He talked through the intercom, "Karen, Carmen is here." Karen responded; "Okay, I will be right out." He introduced Karen and Carmen. She is the owner of Boshae` Boutique. I asked her to come over tonight to give you a "Private Show" of her fall merchandise. Karen looked surprised and said, "Jack, it's extremely nice of you to arrange this "Private Show. How did you meet Carmen?" He hesitated before answering. I met Carmen through a client who shops frequently at her boutique. Carmen gave the impression of being exaggeratedly friendly with Karen, "Jackson came into the boutique today requesting a show, and fortunately, I had availability for tonight!" Karen appeared surprised. "So, you are calling Jack, "Jackson". He hates that name. Carmen replied, "Jackson, why didn't you tell me; you didn't like that name" – she knew; he preferred to be called Jack. He responded, "Jackson is okay as long as I don't hear it on a regular basis. Hearing it from my wife would be more than I could endure."

Carmen stared at Jackson; will you help me get the outfits from my car? He opened her car door and reached for her hand. He moaned, "AAAAAAAAAAAHHHHHHHHH, my cock is SOOOOOOOOOOOOOOO hard. After the show, do you mind participating in a threesome?" She stared angrily at him, Jackson; I'm getting in my car and driving home right now if you don't stop this bullshit. I'm here for one reason only. He softly laughed. "Why are you always so serious?" He smiled at her. "Why don't I come to your home at about 10:00 P.M?" No Jackson Harper! You are not welcome at my home! She glared at her watch; this show is booked for only one hour, so we should get started really soon.

They returned inside the house placing all the outfits and shoes on the den couch. He seemed anxious as he talked with Karen; "I would like to video record you so please let me know when you are coming downstairs – so I can get the recorder ready." Karen shook her head. I like that idea! Carmen stared angrily at Jackson, "What is he up to?" She handed Karen a purple dress and a pair of purple and black pumps. Karen dashed upstairs to try on the outfit.

Jackson kissed Carmen. "UUUUUMMM," he moaned while caressing her tits and back. He unzipped his pants and removed his cock placing Carmen's hand on his hard throbbing stiff cock. She stroked his cock extremely firm. He moaned, "UUUUUUUUMMMMMMMMMMMMM, AAAAAAAAAAAAAHHHHHHHHHHHH, SSSSSSSSSSSSSSSHHHHHHHHHHHHH, YEEEEEEEEEEEEEEEEEESSSSSSSSSSSSSS, AAAAAAAAAAAAHHHHHHHHHHHHH."

Karen announced; "Jack, I'm coming downstairs." He moaned, "Shit, not now Karen. Please give me a few minutes to setup the camera!" He quickly fixed his clothes; "AAAAAHHH, his cock throbbed against his thigh as Karen walked downstairs." As he recorded her, he said, "Gosh Karen! You look so beautiful tonight." Carmen gawked intently at Karen; you look absolutely stunning. Karen extended her arms – spinning around in circles. Jack, would you like to see me model another outfit. Sure Karen! I would love to see you in everything. He hugged Karen as Carmen handed her another outfit. Karen moaned, "OOOOHHHHH," as she fixed her eyes on at the red pants suit and black wing back pumps. Karen said, "Gosh! I already like this outfit and color. Red is Jackson's favorite color!" He was becoming impatient with Karen, since his cock was throbbing against his thighs. As soon as Karen went upstairs, he unzipped his pants and removed his hard throbbing cock. OOOOOOHHHHHH, Carmen please suck my cock? "No, Jackson not here!" Please don't say, "No!" I want to feel your hot mouth sucking my cock. OOOOOOOHHHHHH, Carmen leaned over and sucked Jackson's cock "UUUUUUMMMMMMMMMMMM, AAAAAAAAAAHHHHHHHHHHHHHH, SSSSSSSSSSSSHHHHHHHHHHHHHH, YEEEEEEEEEEEEESSSSSSSSSSSSSSSSSSSS, EEEEEEEEEEEEEEEERRRRRRRRRRRRRRR."

As she sucked his cock, he moaned and groaned, "Don't stop!" His groaning was getting extremely louder. "AAAAAAAAAAAAAAHHHHHHHHHH, SSSSSSSSSSSSSSSSHHHHHHHHHHHHHH," Karen asked, "Jack, did you say something?" He responded, "How are things coming along?" I will be down in five minutes. He moaned," AAAAHHHHHH, we have five minutes." Carmen firmly stroked his cock with her hand. He moaned, "SSSSSSSSSHHHHHHHHH." Karen announced; I'm coming downstairs. He rushed fixing his clothing.

When Jackson saw Karen, he whispered, "You look awesome, Baby." Karen thanked him and said, "One more outfit for tonight." He smiled at Carmen while she shook her head okay. Jackson said, "Okay, Karen one more." Carmen gave Karen a black jumpsuit with a black and white jacket with matching black and white pumps. Carmen said, "Karen, please pin your hair off your shoulders." Okay, I will try my best. It might take a while. He kissed Karen. Take your time; Carmen and I don't mind waiting. She returned upstairs. As soon as Karen walked upstairs, Jackson unzipped his pants. "UUUUUUUMMM."

He kissed Carmen; that was smart thinking. He whispered, "I want you to sit on my throbbing cock." She hesitated, no Jackson! "You are out of your mind!" No, I want you to fuck my cock with your hot wet pussey. No Jackson, you have gone to far! He sighed, "Carmen, I know you don't have time to remove your nylons." She said, "Sure, I do Jackson!" Carmen, please stop teasing me. She kissed him. I'm not teasing you. He moaned, "SSSSSSSHHHHHHH," as he sat on the couch and removed his cock from his pants. She stood in front of him lifting up her dress. She moaned, "EEEEEEEEEERRRRRRRR," am I teasing you? I want to fuck your hard cock. "UUUUMMMMMMMM." She squat down over his hard throbbing cock, Baby; are you removing your panties. No, there is no need too! I'm wearing crouchless panties. "AAAHHHHHHHHHHH, Carmen, your pussey feels GOOOOOOOOD." Carmen slid her pussey on Jackson's cock while slowing standing up and slowly sitting down. He moaned, "UUUUUUUMMMMMMM, I never thought fucking could be so great." He began moving his ass back and forth on the couch; he yelled loud, "Shit Carmen! AAAAAAAAHHHHHHHHH, please fuck me!" Karen yelled downstairs, "Did you say something, Jack?" Sure, I asked are you almost ready? Give me another three minutes. He yelled, "Hold on, Baby until I get the camera." Karen walked downstairs while Carmen stood at the foot of the stairs. Carmen sighed, "Karen, you really look stunning and your hair is marvelous." Karen eagerly wanted to see the other outfits. She said, "This is so much fun." Jackson gave the impression of being well entertained and said, "Yes Karen, this is SOOOOOOOOO much fun!" Well Karen, I have two evening dresses, a jean jumpsuit, and three casual dresses. Karen smiled. I will try one of the evening dresses; perhaps, I will convince Jack to take me out on the town. He hugged her, sure anything for you want. Karen took the dress and shoes upstairs. He took Carmen by the hand; let's finish where stopped. She said, "No Jackson, we should stop now. We're skating on extremely thin ice!" Shit, my cock is throbbing; I want you to stroke it with your pussey! She hesitated; okay Jackson, sit down. We should make this quick before we get caught. As soon as Carmen slid her pussey on his cock, Karen said, "I'm coming downstairs." Jack moaned, "OOOOHHHHHHH, SSSSSSSSSSHHHHHHHHHHHHHHH,

AAAAAAAAAAAAAAAAAAAAHHHHHH, Carmen, fuck me." He moved his ass faster and faster on the couch. Her pussey felt so hot too him, "AAAAAAAAAAHHHHHHHHHHHHHH; OOOOOOOOOHHHHHHHHHHH Baby, please fuck me." She announced Jack; "I'm coming downstairs." Carmen demanded; 'No Jackson, stop now'! He stood from the crouch appearing extremely irritated. He sprayed air freshener in the room before Karen walked downstairs. Karen was as beautiful in the evening dress as in the other outfits.

Gosh Karen! Jackson was right when he said, "Purple is particularly pretty color on you. I have two purple sweaters at the boutique." Okay Carmen, I will stop by on Friday! She dashed upstairs to change; she returned downstairs and said, "I would like to buy everything Jack." Sure Karen, we will buy everything. She hugged him, "Jack, what am I feeling?" He pretended, come on Karen you are embarrassing me. Oh sorry Jack! I almost forgot that Carmen is here with us. Carmen thought, "Trust me, Jackson haven't forgotten." He thanked Carmen for the "Private Show." He smirked at Karen; too bad you didn't try on every outfit. Carmen shook Jackson's hand; "The main thing is Karen was simply dazzling tonight." Carmen thanked Jackson and Karen for their time. Karen said, "Thank you Carmen for coming here tonight. Now, I will shop at your boutique more frequently." Carmen smiled at Jackson. "I will mail the bill to your office." He smiled at her. "Why don't you stay for dinner?" Karen agreed, "That's an excellent idea!" Carmen picked up her purse; thanks, but I really must leave. He gave her a half smile and said, "I will expect the bill in the mail." She said, "Goodnight. It's a pleasure meeting you, Karen." Jackson opened Carmen's car door; "Can, I stop by later?" No Jackson, you cannot! He closed her car door; I will call you later to say, "Goodnight." Goodnight Jackson. Goodnight Baby.

She drove home thinking about her night at the Harper's. She began regretting how she and Jackson behaved earlier. She said, "Damn! Why did I allow myself to get out of control like that? I can't continue behaving this way with Jackson because it seems as if he has no shame in whatever he does, and I find myself acting as disrespectful as him. Shit! I'm responsible for my own actions, so I can't blame Jackson for my behavior. Tears rolled down her face, I would hate if another lady came into my house behaving the way I did tonight. So what make me believe Karen would be accepting of my behavior in her house."

As she opened her house door, the phone ranged, she rushed over and answered the phone. Hello. Hi Carmen, it's Jessie. Hi Jessie, "How are you doing?" Fine Baby, "Where have you been, I have been calling all evening?" Oh, I gave a "Private Show" over at the

Harper's home tonight? He cruelly responded, "What Carmen? Did you say, "Jackson Harper? Have you lost your mind?" She was feeling really bad; I gave his wife Karen a "Private Show" tonight and that's it. His spoke to her extremely harsh, "I don't believe Carmen; you went over to that women's house when you know; you are involved in a "Forbidden love affair" with her husband." Oh, Jessie calm down. Everything turned out great! He leaned against his bedroom wall, "Great for you but what happens if Karen ever finds out that you are fucking her husband." She was getting angry; Jessie, why are you so positive that 'I've had an affair with Karen's husband? You really should mind your business. He asked, "Carmen, why are you getting so entangled with Jackson? Was he that great of a fuck?" She snapped, "No Jackson!" Tears rolled down her face. Gosh! I apologize Jessie. I didn't mean to call you Jackson, but he is so much fun. He cleared his throat; am I not fun to you? Yes Jessie! "But, Jackson tells me what he wants and feels? You hesitate too much on expressing your feelings. You beat around the bush expecting that I will read your mind. Right now in my life Jessie, I want the spontaneousness and Jackson is every bit of that until it almost feels dangerous." Jessie, you are still living through Pauline after so many years. You continue telling me that you are not happy, but you are not doing anything differently to change your current circumstances. Jackson hasn't told me once that he isn't happy with his wife. If he was truly unhappy, I don't believe he would still be there. He did admit when I first met him that he wasn't sexually attracted to her, but he didn't say that he didn't love her nor did he feel trapped in the marriage. Jessie, how many times have I told you that you must do whatever makes you happy? Yes! I enjoyed making love to you, but I also enjoyed spending time with Jackson. Jessie, you can't tell me that you don't enjoy spending time with Shirley. There is more to you staying with her than an outdated commitment; you have made with Pauline. He said, "So you enjoy spending your time with a perfect stranger than with someone you have known for years?" Please leave Jackson name out of our conversation for once.

He sighed, "I'm getting horny; I'm on my way over." No Jessie not tonight! But are you busy on Friday or Saturday?" He coughed, "I don't know for sure, but I will call you later in the week to let you know." Shirley's best friend is celebrating her birthday at Spencer's Restaurant and Lounge on Friday. Oh, Liz and I have plans to meet at Spencer's on Friday night. Jessie, I will see you at Spencer's on Friday. I need to go now. Have a goodnight!

She dialed Liz's number. Hi Liz, it's Carmen. Carmen, "How did it go tonight?" Karen liked everything; she was absolutely stunning. Yes Liz! She and Jackson purchased everything. Liz appeared distracted. Carmen asked, "Liz are you okay?" Yes Carmen, I have company! Liz, "Why didn't you say something earlier? I will talk with you at the boutique on tomorrow."

The phone ranged, Carmen thought; I should let it ring; but perhaps, it's Jackson. Hello. Hi Baby, I'm calling to thank you again and to say, "Goodnight." Hi Jackson. He began moaning, "UUUUMMM," I want to come over. She quickly responded, "No Jackson, please stop – not right now!"

I'm not feeling too great. He whispered, "I can come over too make you feel much better." She angrily responded, "No Jackson! I believe you and I should be ashamed of our behavior tonight at your home. I don't know if you really enjoy living your life on edge, but I will not live this way. My morality will not allow me to continue behaving this way." He became extremely quite. She asked, "Are you still here?" Yes Carmen! He sighed, "I apologize you are feeling ashamed of our behavior tonight. Perhaps, we should analyze our behavior but if it feels incredible why stop. Shit Carmen! We both deserve to be happy." No Jackson, "Not if Karen gets hurt during the process! Happiness is based upon true feelings, commitment, honesty, and integrity. I truly believe; our relationship doesn't possess any of those characteristics!"

She changed the subject, "How is Karen?" She's the happiest she has been in a long time. She hasn't mentioned her illness, since I have returned home. My love is growing stronger everyday for Karen, and it's all attributed to you, Carmen. She and I are flying out on Friday at 4:35 P.M; I would like for you to join Karen and me. No Jackson, I'm not flying anywhere this weekend with you! "Five minutes ago, you mentioned that your love is growing stronger for Karen, and you are still recruiting for threesomes." He sighed, "I know that you are totally against threesomes, but you can't blame me for trying." Jackson, I hope you and Karen have a great weekend. He moaned, "UUUUUUUMMMMMMM, it would be even better if you would join us." No Jackson, I really mean no! So please never mention this to me again. Okay, if you change your mind, please call or meet me at the airport. Karen yelled, "Jackson, who are you talking with?" He responded; "Baby, I'm making reservations for this weekend." Carmen, I must go now but thank you very much for tonight. You are so welcome Jackson. Goodnight! While getting dressed for bed, she thought; "What a day, hopefully tomorrow isn't as wild as today."

Chapter Four

A Day at the Cabin

As Carmen rolled over in bed her alarm clock sounded. She glanced at the clock; damn, morning came so quickly! "UUUUUUUMMMMMMMM," I will rest for another fifteen minutes before getting up. While resting in bed, her phone ranged. Hello. Good morning Carmen, it's Randolph. Good morning, Randolph. "How did you get my home telephone number?" I got it from Ruth's address book. "Randolph, what the hell is wrong with men snooping in a woman's address book?" He seemed confused by her question, what was that Carmen? She didn't answer.

He sounded so sneaky; Carmen will you have lunch with me today? Sure Randolph! What restaurant should I meet you? I would prefer having lunch with you at my cabin. Ruth and I have a cabin off Mountain Crest Road. No Randolph! That's a two-hour drive, and I don't have time to drive there today. I have several appointments, so I really should be at the boutique today. "UUUUUUMM," Carmen, could I call you later? Yes Randolph, you can call around – 9:00 A.M! Okay Carmen! I will talk with you later.

She got out of bed saying, "It's starting to be another wild and crazy day." She arrived at the boutique. Good morning Carmen. Good morning Liz, "How are you feeling?" Carmen, "I'm feeling marvelous." Thanks for asking. Carmen glanced at the clock and asked, "How many appointments do we have scheduled for today?" Carmen, we have five appointments today. Also, Mrs. Smith called ten minutes ago. Gosh! Liz why so early? She wanted to know if you have time for a "Private Show" today. She apologized for calling with such short notice, but she had surgery on her face one week ago and doesn't want to be seen in public right now. Her face is still swollen. The phone ranged. Liz go ahead and prepare for the first appointment, I will answer the phone. "Boshae`. Hi Mrs. Smith. Yes, I can arrive there at about 11:00 A.M!" Good-bye Mrs. Smith. As she walked away from the counter, the phone ranged again. "Boshae`, Carmen speaking. Hello Carmen, it's Randolph. Can I see you today?" Sure! I have a "Private Show" scheduled with Mrs. Smith today at 11:00 A.M. "They live north of Mountain Crest Road." He promptly asked, "This isn't Audrey and Keith Smith?" No Randolph, this isn't Audrey Smith! But, she is one of my clients. Randolph is 1:00 P.M. a great time! His voice sounded excited; that time is magnificent. He gave her the street address and phone number. Carmen, the cabin sets really far from the street, so there's a possibility you might overlook it.

Carmen walked into her office. A few minutes later Liz walked out into the boutique, Carmen, I spoke with Mrs. Smith, and she would like for you to bring a few evening dresses, winter business suits, and casual outfits. She and Mr. Smith are taking a trip to buy "Paintings and Sculptures" for their Art Gallery. Liz, go ahead and select a few items, and I will drive them over to Mrs. Smith's home. I may not return prior to you closing this evening, but I will definitely meet you at Spencer's. Liz smirked, what time would you be at there tonight? Liz, around eightish." By the way Carmen, "Who were you talking to earlier on the phone?" Oh, an old friend who also resides off Mountain Crest Road. I'm planning to stop by once; I finish at Mrs. Smith's home. Carmen, it sounded as if you already had plans. Only partially, I wasn't really sure whether I would be able to stop by today. So, "Who is this friend Carmen?" Liz, you are full of questions this morning. They both gleefully laughed as Carmen walked out the door. She yelled to Liz, "I will see you at Spencer's tonight!"

Carmen arrived at Mrs. Smith home in a fabulous mood. Mrs. Smith greeted Carmen at the door introducing her to Mr. Smith. Carmen, Mr. Smith surprised me by coming home early today for this "Private Show." I don't recall telling him, but here he is. Carmen smiled. "Mr. Smith, it's great that you came home early – this show will be an incredible treat for you."

Mrs. Smith, Liz, choose outfits she knew will look stunning on you. Mrs. Smith agreed; Liz really has an awesome gift for picking out the perfect outfits for me. Carmen asked, "Can I help you carry these things upstairs or would you prefer changing in here." No Carmen! Why don't you and Mr. Smith come into the bedroom while I change! Sure! Mr. Smith helped Carmen carry the outfits upstairs to their bedroom. Carmen glanced around the bedroom, Mrs. Smith this is such a lovely room. "UUUUUUMMMM," Mr. Smith and I've had great times in here. Mr. Smith stared at Carmen and winked his eyes. Carmen said, "Mrs. Smith, can we get started; I have another appointment within one hour." Sure thing Carmen, but you are always so busy!

It occurred to Carmen that Mrs. Smith's first name is Audrey. Carmen thought, "I should find out Mr. Smith's first name." She momentary glanced at Mrs. Smith. "I would like to add Mr. Smith to my mailing list, so I can send out gift ideas for special

Holidays." Oh, yes Carmen, where's my manners! "It's Keith." Carmen sighed, "HHHHMMMMM. So, Randolph does know Audrey and Keith Smith. I know Randolph didn't inform Keith that I'm at his house for a "Private Show." The nerve of Randolph; or than again, this may possibly be coincidental."

Mr. Smith whispered, "You look quite lovely today." Thanks Mr. Smith. He moaned, "HHHHHHMMMM, I love the way your ass look in those leather pants, and your tits look so sexy in that black sweater." "SSSSSSSHHHHHHHHH." Carmen whispered, "Mr. Smith, Audrey, can hear you." He insisted. No, she cannot! She is only worried about how she looks until she has forgotten about my needs. "UUUUUUUUMMMMMMMMMMM, it sure would be nice if you could sit your cunt on my face. I want to slide my tongue over your clit until you scream for more. AAAAAAAHHHHHHHHHH, UUUUUUUUUUUUUUUMMMMMMMM." Stop Mr. Smith, you are making me feel extremely horny. He licked his lips; go on Carmen enjoy this wonderful feeling. He moaned, "AAAAARRRRR, visualize me sliding my throbbing cock into your pussey." He unzipped his pants and removed his hard stiff cock. Mr. Smith, Audrey, will catch you with your cock hanging from your pants. He moaned, "AAAAARRRRRR, she will be in the mirror for at least ten minutes." Carmen agreed, that sounds like

Mrs. Smith; she really enjoys looking at herself in the mirror, but please put your cock back inside your pants. He walked over to Carmen, and placed her hand on his cock. "AAAAAAAHHHHHHHHHHHHH, SSHHHHHHHHHHH. Carmen, please stroke my throbbing cock." She stroked his cock extremely firm and gravely slow. "AAAAAAAHHHHHHHH," Mr. Smith whispered, "My cock is so hard. Damn! Don't stop Carmen." Mrs. Smith yelled; "Eat your hearts out darling as she opened the bathroom door." When she entered into the bedroom, Mr. Smith quickly turned – walking from the bedroom with his cock dangling from his pants. Keith, don't you want to see how lovely; I look in this outfit. "Sure Audrey, in one moment!" He returned into the bedroom after placing his cock back into his pants. He said, "Gosh Audrey! You really look magnificent. Carmen doesn't Audrey looks smashing in this outfit." Carmen smiled. "Yes, Mrs. Smith really does look stunning! Should I repack this outfit or do you have plans to purchase it?" Keith quickly responded, "Carmen, we will purchase this outfit."

Mrs. Smith wait until you catch sight of the next outfit. I bought your favorite color in a pair of leather pants. Audrey try these pants so, Mr. Smith can get a glimpsed of how sexy you are. He said, "Hopefully as sexy as you." Carmen smiled at him; "She will." Mrs. Smith excitedly said, "Give me ten minutes as she closed the bathroom door." Mr. Smith walked over to Carmen and kissed her lips. He caressed Carmen's tits as he slowly slid his tongue into her mouth. "SSSSSSSSSSSHHHHHHHH, AAAAAAAAAAAAAHHHHHHHHHHHH" Carmen lifted her sweater as Keith firmly caressed her tits. He bent down and passionately sucked her tits as he caressed his hands back and forth over her ass. She lowered her sweater and said, "Keith, Audrey is dressed, so we should stop now." As Carmen walked over too the window, Mrs. Smith walked from the bathroom wearing the red leather pants. Keith moaned, "UUUUUUMMMMMMM. Audrey, you look absolutely great in those red leather pants." Mrs. Smith licked her lips as she moaned, "SSSSSSSSHHHHH, Keith. OOOOOHHHH, AAAAAAAAAAAAAHHHHH, darling." He moaned and groaned, "EEEERRRRRR, UUUUUUMMMMMMM, SSSSSSSSHHHHH," as she caressed her body against his body. Audrey whispered, "Keith your cock is so hard, if I knew leather would make you so horny, I would have purchased an outfit years ago." She slowly kissed him, and stroked her hand over his throbbing cock. Audrey moaned and groaned, "KEEEIIIITTTHHH, I want too feel your cock," but we have company. "UUUUUUUUUUMMMMMM," he kissed her lips and whispered, "I know Carmen will enjoy watching.

AAAAAAAAAAAAAAAAHHHHHHHHHHHH." Mrs. Smith removed her sweater while Mr. Smith caressed her tits. They both were breathing exceptionally hard. "SSSSSSSSHHHHHH."

Mrs. Smith moaned, "OOOOOHHHHH KEEEEIIIIIITTTTTTTTTHHHHHHHH." Carmen was beginning to feel incredibly horny, but she said, "Mr. & Mrs. Smith. I have another appointment." Gosh Carmen! "We're extremely sorry; we were getting beside ourselves." Mrs. Smith removed her pants; I will try the evening dress now. Mr. Smith caressed her ass. She moaned, "No Keith, Carmen is in a hurry!" She slipped into a black evening dress. Gosh Carmen! This is the perfect special occasion black dress. Keith moaned, "Come here Audrey, I can't believe how lovely you look. AAAAAAAAAAAAHHHHHHHHH Baby, I'm SOOOOOOOOOOOOOOOOOOOO, glad I'm here. UUUUUUUUUMMMMMM, Audrey, I didn't know trying on clothing could be so exciting." She excitedly asked, "Carmen, when can we book another appointment?" Carmen glimpsed at her watch, "Audrey, please call Liz to schedule an appointment."

Audrey smiled at Keith. "We will purchase six of these outfits today." Mr. Smith, I will mail you the bill in a few days. Carmen hugged Audrey and said, "Mr. Smith please have a magnificent weekend, and have fun with those red leather pants." Mr. Smith excitedly smiled. That's the plan once you leave. He carried the remaining outfits to Carmen's car. He thanked Carmen for the "Private Show." She smiled. He said, "I don't want you to leave. I wish, you could have watched or joined Audrey and me fucked. I look forward to seeing you again."

Carmen drove into the direction of the Jenkins' cabin, but she first stopped by the store. She asked the clerk, "If there was a public restroom?" Sure Madam! "Straight in the back." She was wearing her red trench coat and decided to surprise Randolph by removing all of my clothing and only wear her red trench coat and red pumps. As she was walking out the store, she spotted a can of cool whip and jar of cherries. "HMMMMMMMMMMMMMMMMMMMMM, I will buy these items to have fun with Randolph."

She arrived at the cabin with no problems. She ranged the doorbell carrying a brown paper sack. Randolph opened the cabin door wearing only his briefs. Hello Carmen, I'm so glad that you were able to stop by this afternoon. He closed the door taking her into his arms while he excitedly kissed her lips. He moaned with exceedingly roaring sounds, "UUUUUUUMMMMMM, I waited all morning to feel you in my arms, and this is exactly how I thought it would be."

He kissed her as he moaned, "AAAAAAAHHAAHHHHHHHHHHHH. You smell so awesome, Carmen." Randolph untied her coat belt and discovered; she was totally naked underneath her trench coat. OOOOOHHHHH, Carmen, Randolph whispered, "My cock is throbbing. AAAAAAAAAAAAHHHHHHHHHHHHH, UUUUUUUUUUUUMMMMMMMMMMMM, AAAAAAAAAAAAAHHHHHHHHHHHH, Baby, your body feels so great! AAAAAAAHHHHHHHHHHHHHHHHH, I'm SOOOOOOOOOOOOOOOOOOOO glad you are here with me." He held her in his arm; thanks for being here with me.

He attentively stared into her eyes and kissed her; then escorted her over to the bed. He slowly kissed her lips while rubbing his hands all over her body. He slid his tongue down her stomach until he reached her pussey. "AAAAAAAHHHHHHHHH, Randolph that FEEEEEEEEEEEELS GOOOOOOOOOD." She whispered, "Randolph, your tongue is SOOOOO hot. AAAAAAAAAAAAAAAAHHHHHHHH, OOOOOOOOOOOOOOHHHHHHHHH, Randolph don't stop! UUUUUUUUMM, you are so GOOOOOOOOOOOOOD." He slowly fucked Carmen's pussey with his tongue, "AAAAAAAAAAAAHHHHHHHH," Randolph whispered, "Your PUUUSSSSEEEEEEYYYYYYY taste GOOOOOOOOOOOOOOOOD" AAAAAAAAAAAHHHHHHHHHHHHH, Baby, I want to fuck your pussey." Carmen sat up in bed whispering, "Not now Randolph." She kissed his lips. He moaned and groaned while moving his ass back and forth on the bed. "AAAAAAAAAAAAAAAHHHHHHHHHHH, Carmen YEEEEEEEEEEEEEEEESSSSSSSSS, Baby. AAAAAAAAAAAAAAAAHHHHHHHHHHH, I want your pussey now." She unzipped his pants and began stroking his hard throbbing cock while she removed his pants. She got out of bed and walked over to the table. She removed the brown bag, and carried it over to the table. As she removed the cool whip, he stared at her in amazement. He moaned and groaned, "UUUUUUUMMMMMMMMMM, Carmen, what are you planning to do with the cool whip? SSSSSSSSSSSSSSSHHHHHHHHHH, AAAAAAAAAHHHHHHHHHHHHHHH."

She removed the cap from the cool whip and sprayed it all over his hard stiff cock. "AAAAAAAAAHHHHHHHHHHHHHH," he moaned as he glanced at his cock. Carmen opened the jar of cherries and placed two onto the head of his cock. His cock pointed straight in the air while she licked off the cool whip. He moaned and groaned, "EEEEEEEEERRRRRRR," while breathing out of control. He moved his ass back and forth on the bed really getting into the groove of having his cock sucked. He whispered, "AAAAAAAAAAHHHHHHH, CARMEEEEEEEEEENNNNNNNN suck my throbbing cock. AAAAAHHHHHHH, please suck my throbbing cock." She leaned over his throbbing cock, slowly licking her tongue over his cock. "SSSSSSSSSSHHHHHHHH, CARMEEEEEN. AAAAAAAAAAAAHHHHHHH, that feels SOOOOOOOOOOOOOOOOOOOOOOO OO GOOOOOOOOOOOOOOOOOD." She removed a cherry in her mouth and slid in the bed until her mouth reached his mouth; she dropped the cherry into his mouth. "AAAAAAAAAAAAAAAHHH, UUUUUUUUUUUMMM," she removed the other cherry with her mouth from his cock, sliding her body to his mouth and dropping the last cherry into his mouth. "AAAAAAAHHHHHHHHHHH, EEEEEEEEEEEEEEEERRRRRRRRRRRRRRR, I'm SOOOOOOOOOOO horny." Carmen sucked the cool whip from his cock. He screamed with excitement, "AAAAAAAAAAHHHHHHH. Carmen, this feels SOOOOOOOOOOOOO GOOOOOOOOOOOOO." She licked the remaining cool whip from his cock, and placed her tongue into his mouth as he sucked the cool whip from her tongue. AAAAAAAHHHHHHHHH, he moaned. He was really turned-on by the cool whip and cherries on his hard throbbing cock. "UUUUUUUUUUUMMMMMM, I love how you sucked my cock, CARMEEEEEEEEEEEN. EEEEEEEEERRRRRRRRRRRR. Gosh Carmen! Your mouth feels SOOOOOOOOOOOOOO GOOOOOOOOOOOOOOOOOOOOD."

He was getting so excited until he slightly sat up in bed watching her dress his cock with the cool whip and cherries. She placed three cherries on his throbbing cock while he moved his ass back and forth on the bed. "AAAAAAAAAHHHHHHHHH Carmen, my cock look SOOOOOOOOOOOO delicious with the cool whip and cherries. OOOOOOOOOOHH, my cock feels as if it will exploded all over the room." She passionately licked the cool whip from his cock and slid her body in bed until her mouth reached his mouth slowing sticking her tongue into his mouth. "SSSSSSSSSHHHHH," he slowly sucked the cool whip from her tongue. They both moaned and groaned, "AAAAAARRRRRRR, EEEEEEEEEEEEERRRRRRRRRRRRRRRRR, SSSSSSSSSHHHHHHHHHHHHHHH," while holding each other so incredibly tight. He moaned, "Carmen feed me the cool whip from my cock." She slid in bed and steadfastly stuck her tongue into his mouth as he vigorously sucked the cool whip from her tongue. "AAAHHHHHHHHHHHH, Baby, that feels and taste GREEEEEEAAAAAAAAAT!"

She took a cherry into her mouth and slid in bed dropping the cherry into his mouth. "AAAAAAAAAAAAAAAAHHHHHHHHH HHHHHHH, Baby, shit, I'm so excited until I can't take anymore of this. She ate the other two cherries from his cock and finish eating the cool whip. EEEEEEEEEEEEEEERRRRRRRRRRRRRRRR, AAAAAAAAAAAAAAHHHHHHHHHH," I want to eat cool whip from your cunt. "UUUUUUUUUMMMMMMMMMMMMM, OOOOOOOOOOOHHHHHHHHHHHHH, OOOOOOOOOOOOHHHHHHHHHHHH, YEEEEEEEEEEEESSSSSSSSSSSS, Randolph, I want you to eat cool whip from my cunt." She rested on her back as Randolph seemed to be so excited as he firmly caressed her cunt with his physically powerful hands. "UUUUUUUUUSUUUUUMMMMMMMM MMMMMMM, AAAAAAAHHHHHHHH," he slowly caressed his tongue back and forth over her clit. She pressed her cunt firmly against his tongue. He stopped and sprayed the cool whip over her cunt. "OOOOOOOOOOOOOOOHHHHHHHH, RANDOLLLLLLPH eat my pussey." I want to feel your tongue sliding against my clit. Shit, RANDOLLLLLLPH don't stop! She sat up slightly in bed as she watched him eat the cool whip from her cunt. He had cool whip all over his face. She whispered, "Come here; she slowly licked his face as he held her extremely firm in his arms." He moaned and groaned with excitement, "AAAAAAHHH, SSSSSSSSSSSSHHHHHHH. I want to fuck your hot wet cunt. I want to feel my throbbing cock sliding in and out of your cunt." He slid his throbbing cock into her cunt. "OOOOOOOOHHHH. MY, MY, MY, MY Carmen, your cunt is incredible. AAAAAAAAAAAAAHHHHHHHH, Carmen, fuck me; fuck me." She began fucking his cock harder and faster as he screamed, "AAAAAAAAAHHHHHHHHHHHHH." She continued sliding her ass on the bed faster and faster as his sweat dripped all over her body. He moaned and groaned, "EEEEEEEEEEEERRRRRRRRRRR." His breathing was getting louder and louder. The sweat was dripping faster as he moved his cock back and forth into her cunt. His body began to jerk, "AAAAAAAAHHHHHHHHHHHHHHHH, shit Carmen! I'm CUUUUMMIIIINNNGGGG. Don't stop moving Carmen! Please take all of my CUUUUUUUUUUUUUUUMMMMMMM into your hot wet juicy cunt. EEEEEEEEEERRRRRRRRRR, please Baby take all of my CUUUUUUUUUUMMMM. AAAAAAAAAAHHHHHHHHH, your cunt is SOOOOOOOO GOOOOOOOOOOOOD. Baby, Baby, Baby your cunt is like a burning inferno." He kissed her and said, "Baby, you are really,

"HOOOOOOOOOOOT." She kissed him; I need to drive back before Liz closes the boutique. He whispered, "Thank you so much for stopping by. I really enjoyed everything, and I hope we can spend time together again soon." She cleared her throat, "Randolph, I can't make any promises to you." He kissed her shoulder. I promise you; it will be worth your time.

He fixed his eyes on her; Carmen, have you ever thought about having a "Fashion Show" at the boutique! No Randolph, I can't say that I have! He smiled. "I really believe; it would go over remarkably well." She smiled at him, "Why do you say that Randolph?" He rubbed his hands over his chest. "Your clients really like shopping at your boutique and why not sponsor a "Fashion Show" for your clients and have them model the outfits." Carmen, this show will bring a gargantuan profit into Boshae`." She raised her hands into the air; Randolph, why didn't I think of this idea earlier! He smiled. "Carmen, the husband will spend money at the "Fashion Show" because most of them enjoy buying lavish gifts for their wives." She got out of bed. Randolph, you are right about that. You can expect an invitation in the mail really soon to attend a "Fashion Show" at Boshae`. Of course, Ruth will be one of the models and so will Audrey Smith.

By the way Randolph, you were right! "About what Carmen?" She smiled. "About Keith and Audrey

Smith." Audrey was surprised that Keith came home early. I wonder, what made him leave his office early today. Randolph said, "Extremely small world." She smirked. "Yes Randolph! Extremely small world!" She quickly showered and returned into the bedroom. He walked over to her and said, "When can I see you again?" She hugged him, "At the, "Fashion Show." I will mail you and Ruth an invitation. Okay. Carmen thanks for the lovely day, and I look forward to seeing soon. Thank you Randolph for the great idea. Bye. Bye-Carmen.

Carmen arrived at the boutique while Liz was preparing to close. Hi Liz, "How was your day?" Fantastic Carmen! Mrs. Carlos purchased three evening gowns and Ms. Williams purchased another fur coat for her mother. Liz, you wouldn't believe what I thought of while driving home. I thought about Boshae` sponsoring a "Fashion Show" for our clients. Liz, stared at Carmen extremely puzzled and repeated "Fashion Show." Yes Liz! The women who shops frequently here at the boutique will model. Our mailing list would be extensive, since our clientele is exceptionally large. You know Carmen; that's a great idea. "Why didn't we think of that sooner?" Liz, that's a notable question, but the main thing is, we are making plans now.

Liz smiled. "Carmen, on Monday, lets began preparing the guess list." Carmen sighed, "Liz, we should consider expanding the boutique to men apparel. We don't have to decide right away but lets stay opened to this idea." Liz sarcastically said, "Carmen, if we opened this boutique to men; it will truly turn into an illegal Brothel." Liz, Boshae` is an extremely respectable boutique, and it will remain that way. Yes, you and I occasionally do things that are not always right, but we will never bring that type of activity here at Boshae`! Now Carmen, "What were you and Jackson doing in your office last week?" They both gently laughed. "Like, I said the other day Liz. Jackson and I were discussing business." Oh Carmen, you are so full of it. Liz quickly replied, "Are you still meeting me at Spencer's tonight?" You bet, Liz! I haven't visited Spencer's in about two months and besides listening to great music always help me to relax. "How was your appointment with Mrs. Smith?" She purchased the two evening dresses and four outfits. Liz said, "Let me guess, she purchased the red leather pants." Yes Liz, and I must admit; Audrey was awfully sexy in those red leather pants; and those red leather pants immensely turned Mr. Smith on. So, was he there at the showing? Yes! Keith was there. That reminds me; I need to reschedule another "Private Show" for Mrs. Smith within one month. Carmen, why don't you wait until the "Fashion Show?" Magnificent idea Liz!

Lets invite at least two hundred guests. Jackson and Karen; oh Jessie and Shirley must attend. I want both Karen and Shirley to model. Jessie mentioned one year ago that he wanted to treat Shirley to a fashion makeover. This "Fashion Show" may possibly be perfect timing for Jessie! Well so much for work, lets go home and dress so that we can let our hair down tonight at Spencer's. I will meet you around eightish. Liz, "What band is playing there tonight?" I'm not sure, but I'm quite sure they are awesome. Yes, you are right or they wouldn't be playing at Spencer's!

Carmen arrived home and shower. While drying her body, the phone ranged. Hello, Hi Carmen, its Jessie. About tonight, I won't be able to spend time with you; Shirley and I are celebrating her best friend Janelle's birthday at Spencer's tonight. Carmen impatiently laughed and said, "Jessie, tell me the real reason why you are calling me. You told me earlier in the week about this party." Carmen, what are you doing tonight? Liz and I have plans to meet at Spencer's! She and I have a night out every third Friday, but I have missed the last two outings. Great! I will see you there. She hastily responded, "Jessie, you will not spy on me while you are entertaining Shirley!" Carmen, "Who said anything about spying on you?" You didn't have to say anything Jessie; I detected it in your voice. She eagerly said, "Jessie, Liz and I are planning a "Fashion Show" in a few months. I would like to have Shirley as one of the model." Great Carmen! Thanks Jessie. I will make sure that I send you an invitation.

I will see you at Spencer's. Carmen dressed thinking, "There will be various acquaintances at Spencer's, and so I must look chic." I wouldn't be surprise if Karen and Jackson weren't there. After all she recently purchased fifteen new outfits. Should I wear black or purple? She amuse herself, "SSSSSSHHHHHH, what about nothing at all?" She moaned, "HHHHMMMMM, I should get serious about getting dress. UUUUUUUUMMM, why don't I wear my red trench coat? Yes, this outfit will be perfect! She got dressed in a black leather skirt and jacket without a bra." She said, "I'm looking extremely stunning if I must say so myself!" Hopefully, this will be the best, "Girls' night out" that I've had in an awfully long time.

Chapter Five

Girls' Night Out

Carmen walked into Spencer's looking smashing. She glanced around trying to locate Liz's table. Liz waved her hand; Carmen walked over hugging her. Liz, you look lovely in this hunter green outfit. Carmen sat in the chair and asked, "Have you met anyone interesting?" No Carmen! I have only been here for approximately ten minutes. Liz bashfully smiled. You wouldn't guess whom I ran into? Who Liz? "Jessie and Shirley." Yes Liz! I spoke with Jessie on yesterday, and he mentioned; he and Shirley would be here tonight. Carmen quickly glanced around the restaurant; where are they sitting? Liz pointed; they are sitting two tables away from the ladies room. Great Liz! I'm on my way to the ladies room. Before excusing herself from the table, she asked, "Liz, how do I look?" Carmen, don't ask – you look fantastic tonight!

As she approached Jessie's table, he almost knocked his drink over. Hi Jessie, I thought I recognized you from my table. "How are you doing tonight?" Fine Carmen. Shirley, this is Carmen Hailey. She is owner and operator of Boshae` Boutique. Carmen extended her hand. "It's a pleasure meeting you, Shirley." She folded her arms; Shirley, I'm having a "Fashion Show" next month and would like for you to model in the show. I have Jessie's mailing address, so I will mail you an invitation. Carmen had an exceptionally big smile on her face; Shirley, I would love for you to become a regular client at the boutique. Shirley appeared exceedingly friendly; Carmen, I have friends meeting me here later, and I will introduce you to them. They all have discussed getting personal makeovers. Okay Shirley, send them my way! As she walked away, she said, "Nice meeting you Shirley and Jessie here tonight."

Carmen quietly laughed as she entered the restroom. "I can't believe Shirley's entire party group are in need of a major fashion makeover. Leave it to me; I will turn them all into beauty queens and showstoppers." She left the restroom strolling leisurely by Jessie's table; he had a twinkle in his eyes. She returned to her table. Carmen, how did Jessie react to your present? He was extremely cordial. I have invited Shirley to participate in the "Fashion Show." Carmen touched Liz hand, guess who just walked in?

Liz asked, "Who Carmen?" She squeezed her index finger, "Jackson and Karen." She said, "Liz, excuse me, but I must go over and tell Karen how smashing she looks tonight." Liz shook her head, "Carmen give them a chance to settle at their table. She stood; Liz, I will be back momentarily.

She approached the Harpers' table. Hi Karen, I noticed you walking in; I want to tell you how smashing you look tonight. She licked her lips; Jackson, "Don't you think so?" He broadly smiled at Karen. "Yes Carmen, Karen looks stunning tonight and so do you!" He stared into her eyes; "Who are you here with?" Carmen smiled. "It's Liz and my "Girls' Night Out." He held both hands together; two sexy women are here alone tonight. "Sure Jackson, and there are also many single sexy men here tonight." He sarcastically said, "That's a shame!" She frowned. "What did you say, Jackson?" He frowned, but didn't respond. She thought, "Jackson, you are so full of bullshit." She touched Karen's hand, "Before I forget, Liz and I'm planning a "Fashion Show" and would like for you too model." Karen briefly glanced at Jackson and then at Carmen; I would love to model. Okay! I will mail an invitation out to you. He asked, "When is this big occasion?" Jackson, I'm unsure of the exact date, but I will keep you and Karen posted. I'm expecting to invite at least one hundred and fifty guests. Karen, if you know anyone interested in attending, please let me know, so I can mail out invitations. Jackson stared at Carmen as he licked his lips. She winked at him and said, "It's great seeing you two here tonight." As Carmen walked away, Jackson said, "Carmen, I will stop by your table later for a dance." Jackson, Karen doesn't approve of her husband dancing with another woman – so goodnight. Enjoy, this time with your wife.

Carmen flagged the Waiter over to her table and said, "I want to buy a round of drinks for the couple sitting next to the piano and the couple sitting two tables away from the ladies room. Tell everyone, the drinks are from Carmen." She thanked the Waiter. Oh, Liz, what are you drinking? Nothing for now, I'm waiting for Melvin to arrive. Great Liz, we need that protection tonight! Liz happily laughed. "Yes Carmen!" Liz, it appears things are going exceptionally well with you and Melvin. "How long has it been, since I have introduced you to Mr. Melvin Kennedy?" It has been eight months, and I'm terrifically glad; you introduced him to me. Carmen amusingly said, "Liz, I'm beginning to notice how sexy Melvin is!" Liz jokingly said, "Keep your hands away from Melvin." Carmen squeezed Liz's arm. Ms. Carlson have you forgotten that I introduced you too him. Liz inquired, "Carmen, when are you planning to meet an eligible bachelor. I hope, it's really soon because if not; you will eventually destroy someone's marriage." Carmen shook her head, "Liz, what are you accusing me of?" Carmen, you know exactly what I'm talking about. You are right Liz; I know exactly what you are talking about – destroying someone's marriage is the last thing on earth; I want to accomplish. Liz glanced at Jackson's table; Carmen, you are on the verge of destroying Jackson and Karen's marriage? Every since you turned forty, your entire attitude has changed. Liz, it's because I know; I'm not getting younger, and I definitely don't want to miss out on anything. Sure Carmen! But, there is so much you can do, so you don't miss out on the pleasures of life at forty, but Sweetie not with someone else's husband. Liz, lets change the subject. This is our "Girl's Night Out," and we will have a blast. Liz sighed. Well Liz, you possibly may not have a blast, but that's my sole purpose for being here at Spencer's tonight." The Waiter returned to the table with Carmen's drink and said, "Everyone thanked you for the rounds of drink." She held her drink in the air slightly as if she was making a toast. Gosh, this Martini hits the spots!

She smiled at Liz; have you eaten dinner? No, I haven't! Liz lets order dinner so if you decide to drink you won't become sick. They walked downstairs to the dinning area. As Carmen and Liz walked downstairs, they met an intriguing gentleman. She and Liz spoke to him and continued walking downstairs. Carmen glanced back and noticed the man staring at her.

"HMMMMMM," Liz, he's remarkably dazzling. "What do you think about him?" Well Carmen, I didn't notice! But, I will once we head back upstairs. After dinner, Carmen asked for the check, but someone had already paid for their dinner. Now, lets head back upstairs, so we can check that brute out. As they walked upstairs, Melvin walked into the door. Liz said, "Hi Melvin, Hi Baby. Melvin, you know Carmen." Yes! Sweetheart you know – I do. Hi Carmen! Hi Melvin, "Now please excuse me; I have someone; I would like to introduce myself too."

She walked over too the tall handsome man standing next too the piano. Hello, my name is Carmen. Hi. I'm Spencer. "UUUUUUMMMM, Spencer?" Yes, I'm the owner! She shook her head. Yes, the name does have similarities! He said, "I couldn't help but notice you as you walked downstairs. Did you and your friend enjoy dinner?" Yes, we did! Someone was nice enough to pay the check. He smiled. I'm that someone. Thanks Spencer. Liz and I thank you very much. I'm Spencer Goodman, and I'm Carmen Hailey. "Are you owner and operator of Boshae` Boutique?" Yes, I'm the one! So, "How are you acquainted with Boshae`?" He smiled, "I shopped there years ago." She smiled. "Now, I remember; you purchased several fur coats." He seemed surprised she remembered. Carmen, you have an exceptional memory. She touched his arm; I will not detain you any longer, Spencer. It's awfully nice meeting you. He said, "No Carmen, the pleasure is all mine!" His voice sounded so sexy! She could feel herself getting extremely excited. "UUUUUUMMMM," she moaned, but I will control myself tonight. As she returned to her table, she encountered three men sitting at a table. One of the man said, "Hello, you look great tonight." She said, "Thanks!" She thought, "I bet these men are here for a quick pickup." One of the men asked, "Can I buy you a drink?" No thanks, perhaps later! I have a drink on my table. Okay, I will send the Waiter over later. She returned to the table and said, "Liz, this is an exceptional Girls' Night Out!" So Carmen, "Who is that attractive man?" He is Spencer. Liz said, "The Spencer." Yes Liz, he is the owner, Spencer Goodman! His last name represents every bit of him. Liz passionately laughed. "Carmen, how did I know you would make that comment?" Liz, "Call it female instinct." Melvin noisily laughed. The Waitress walked over with another Martini for Carmen. It's from Rico Blanco. Carmen asked, "Rico." Yes, he's one of the three gentlemen sitting at the table next too the window! She smiled. Thank him for me! Sure thing and the Waitress walked away. Melvin and Liz went out on the dance floor as Jessie walked over and sat down. He thanked Carmen for the drink; are you having an excellent time tonight Ms. Hailey? YEEEEEEEEEEEEEESSSSS Jessie. He caressed her hand; this leather outfit is a knockout on you. She moved her hand, "Well Jessie, I wanted to turn heads tonight, and I see it's working."

She sipped from her drink; so how is the birthday celebration? He stared at her before answering, "The party is going really well." Shirley is really enjoying herself. "Jessie seemed happy," I haven't seen Shirley have so much fun in such a long time. She really needed this night out. "Gosh Jessie! Jackson said, "The same thing about Karen." Jessie, "Why do you men keep your women's hidden away at home?" Carmen, you know that isn't true with Shirley and me. I know Jessie, you and Shirley have traveled extensively together. He sighed, "Carmen at times, I wished; I was traveling with you." Jessie, don't start with your lies tonight; the alcohol has you saying things that you wouldn't ordinary say. If you wanted me to travel with you, "All you had to do is ask."

He placed his hand underneath his chin; are you enjoying all the attention you are getting tonight. She closed her eyes, all what attention Jessie? I have talked with only two men here tonight. He asked, "Who was the other couple you brought the drinks for?" Jackson and his wife, Karen! He stared Jackson's table with scrutiny, "So, that's Jackson!" He rubbed his hands together. Carmen, I can't wait until we're introduced. No Jessie, not here at the restaurant! Please don't create a disturbance here tonight. He smiled.

"Carmen, I will not create a disturbance here tonight; I'm only going to introduce myself to him. Hell, I have heard so much about him, and I'm also aware that he has a gorilla cock." She hysterically laughed. "Enough Jessie." He amusingly laughed. "Well Carmen, it isn't everyday I have an opportunity to meet another man with a gorilla cock." That's true Jessie but after you meet him, please introduce him too me. He shook his head, "Not on your life, Ms. Hailey." He said, "From a distant Karen is quite lovely." Yes Jessie, she is extremely lovely! He continued looking at Karen, so why is Jackson tip toeing around? Jessie, I don't know; you must ask Jackson for yourself. He said, "Okay, I will before I leave tonight." Jessie, please don't create a disturbance here tonight – don't embarrass Shirley. You are right Carmen! Tonight isn't the best time to meet Jackson, but I will find a way to meet him later. He returned to his table with Shirley.

A few minutes later Jackson walked over to her table. Hi Carmen. Hi Jackson, you look incredibly handsome tonight. "The twinkles in his eyes were surprisingly visible." She smiled. "What are you up to Jackson?" He smiled. "I wanted to say hi and also to tell you; you look really beautiful tonight." Okay Jackson! You have said, "Hi," now please return to your table with your wife. He stared at her, "I would like to take a calculated guess." She asked, "Jackson, about what?" He whispered, "About the gentleman seated here earlier." Jackson, what about him: He whispered, "Was he – Jessie?" Yes Jackson, that was Jessie Hopkins! He placed both hands on the table; I would love for you to introduce us. No Jackson, here isn't the right location or time! It's bad enough; you called Jessie but if you two cause a commotion here tonight; I will never speak to either of you again.

Carmen, you know why I called Jessie. Yes, because you choose not to mind your own business! He affirmed, "You are my business. Jackson, excuse me." He placed both hands onto the table, "Why are you hiding your true feelings? You know; you have fallen in love with me." Jackson, when will you stop flattering yourself? When I first met you, I told you that you were extremely conceited, and it's the honest truth. He enthusiastically laughed. "Carmen, I love it when you get fired up. It makes my cock, SOOOOOOOOOOOOOOOOO hard." He moaned, "AAAAAAAHHHH, I would love to spend time with you tonight." No Jackson, I'm not getting involved with anyone tonight! "Not even with me Carmen." She smiled. "Not even with the man who thinks I'm in love with him." They both mischievously laughed. Jackson noticed Karen returning from the restroom; Carmen, I will talk with you later. Okay, Jackson, but please stay away from Jessie! Okay, Carmen. Promise me Jackson. Carmen, I promise, but I can't control if he walks up to me. You have a point Jackson; have fun with your wife. The entire time while talking with Jackson, she noticed Jessie looking in her direction; but she didn't say anything to avoid creating a disturbance between them.

Rico walked over to the table and asked her to dance. Liz waved her hand when she noticed Carmen and Rico dancing. Rico asked, "Are you married, Carmen?" No! "Do you have any children?" No! " What about you Rico?" Yes, I'm married and have three children! Carmen thought, "Here we go again." I don't want anything else to do with another married man. She asked, "How old are your children?" I have a daughter six and ten, and a son four. She stated; oh, they are all are still babies. "So why aren't you home spending time with your family tonight?" He continued dancing; I occasionally have a night out with my buddies and tonight is my night out. Carmen, I'm glad because I wouldn't have met you. She smiled and thought to herself, "Keep your cock soft buddy until you arrive home to fuck your wife or with someone else, but it will not be with me." As he was moved his body to the music; he said, "Carmen, stop by for a massage." She frowned. "What? Stop by where?" He shook his head; "Oh, pardon me Carmen, I own a Massage Spa – Blanco Massage Retreat. I have clients that spend the entire day at my Spa and really enjoy themselves." She moaned, "HMMMMMM, spending the day at your Spa sounds very intriguing. I haven't treated myself at a Spa in years." He softly moaned, "OOOOOOOOOOOOOOH Carmen, you must visit my Spa, and I will pamper you myself."

He handed her his business card; please give me a call. He asked, "So where do you work?" She smirked. "I'm the owner of Boshae` Boutique." He asked, "On the corner of 5th and Main." She shook her head; so you are acquainted with Boshae`. My wife shops there frequently. Sure! Your wife is Nanita` Blanco. Yes, Nanita` is my wife! She was at the boutique shopping last Saturday. So, I expect to see you and Nanita` at the "Fashion Show." Rico asked, "When is this Carmen?" I haven't decided the precise date, but I will mail out invitations really soon. "I want Nanita` to model in the show." He said, "Great!" Thanks for the dance Rico. She returned to her table. Liz, I'm making so many connections for the "Fashion Show." The man I was dancing with is Nanita` Blanco's husband. He was telling me, "He owned Blanco Massage Retreat, and his wife frequently shopped at Boshae`." Carmen that's great!

She excused herself from the table and headed too the ladies room; as she was returning too her table, she ran into Spencer. He indicated; "SOOOOOO," we meet again Mrs. Hailey. Mr. Goodman, it's Ms. Hailey. "UUUUUUMM, you are not married Carmen?" No and I don't have any children! "What about you Spencer?" He hesitated and said, "No! I'm not married and don't have any children." Carmen couldn't believe her ears. She said to him, "Meeting single men are sometimes quite rare." He said, "Same for meeting single women. Women come here in groups and believe it or not they all are married." She ran her hand through her hair; I bet that haven't stopped you, Spencer. He look as if he was puzzled and said, "Stopped me from doing what?" She moaned, "HHHHHHMMMMMMM," Spencer use your imagination. Without being serious, he asked. "Carmen, do you want an answer?" She shook her head; not right now; perhaps some other time. He moaned, "My cock is throbbing. UUUUMMMM," I'm feeling horny." He walked closer to her; can I kiss you? Before she could answer him, Jackson walked over and stood next to them. Jackson extended his hand, "Hello Spencer." Spencer shook Jackson's hand; "Are you and Karen enjoying your evening?" Carmen thought, "Hell, don't tell me Jackson knows Spencer also. He sure gets around." She glanced at Jackson and said, "Please excuse me." She had this look on her face as if to say, "You really should mind your own business." He stared at her and moved his lips, saying, "I'm watching you." She repeated, "Excuse me Spencer, I will talk with you later." Sure thing, Carmen! Carmen said to Liz, "The nerve of Jackson." Carmen, I couldn't help but notice you and Spencer talking when Jackson interrupted. Oh, Liz, we were only having small talk. Liz glanced at Melvin and than at Carmen. "Carmen, are you and Jackson in a relationship? Since, the first day I met Jackson; I could sense something out of the ordinary happening between the two of you!" Carmen placed both hands underneath her chin, "Liz, I will tell you one day, but tonight isn't the time." Liz warned Carmen, "Please be really careful! Jackson's behavior is becoming extremely dangerously."

Jackson marched over to Liz and Carmen's table. Liz said, "Have a seat Jackson!" He thanked Liz and said, "Carmen, where is your etiquettes?" Sorry Jackson, please have a seat. Liz noticed Melvin walking back to the table and excused herself; I'm going to dance with Melvin." Jackson angrily said, "I'm watching you." She stared at him; what is your damn problem? Jackson, you've had too much to drink. Jessie walked over taking Carmen by the hand onto the dance floor. Carmen could sense Jackson was becoming extremely annoyed by Jessie's boldness; he sat and watched her dance the entire time. Jessie, I hope the alcohol doesn't cause Jackson to create a commotion here tonight.

Jackson came onto the dance floor with Karen; as he danced, he watched Carmen, intensely. When the music finished, he escorted Karen over too Carmen's table. He asked, "Do you mind if Karen and I join you and your friends?" Before, Carmen could answer; he had sat down. He extended his hand to Jessie and said, "I'm Jackson Harper, and this is my wife, Karen." Jessie slightly smiled. "I'm Jessie Hopkins." He shook Jackson and Karen's hands. Jackson smirked and said, "As last we meet Jessie." Before Jessie could answer, Shirley swiftly walked over to the table. Jessie introduced Jackson to Shirley Wilson. Shirley shook his hand and said, "It's really nice meeting you, Jackson." She placed her arm around Jessie's neck, please come back to the table, so we can take pictures. Carmen could sense Jessie was extremely angry; he got up from the table and said, "Jackson, at last we meet." Carmen fixed her eyes on Jackson – thinking, "Please act civilized." He stared into Carmen's eyes while caressing Karen's hand and said, "Carmen, you look dazzlingly lovely tonight?" She said; "Please excuse me, my friend Spencer is standing alone." She stood from the table and walked off leaving Jackson and Karen still sitting there. She noticed the fire in his eyes. She knew he hated her leaving him sitting at the table as she walked over to walk with Spencer.

She approached Spencer, "Why are you standing here alone?" He winked his eye; I knew it would be a magnet to you. She smiled. Yes, it worked! She apprehensively asked; "How long have you known Jackson?" Spencer reached for her hand, about fifteen years. Jackson drew up legal documents for me when I first opened this restaurant. He has also assisted me with other legal matters. She stared into the direction of Jackson's table; does, he come here frequently? Spencer promptly shook his head. No! Jackson spends much of his time at home when he is not traveling. He placed his hands into his pockets. Carmen, I ran into Jackson during numerous business trips; one thing, I'm able to say, since I have known him; he has only been involved with his wife, Karen. She thought to herself; "I have corrupted Jackson." Spencer assertively asked, "How are you acquainted with Jackson?" She debated with herself whether to tell the truth, but she said, "He stopped by the boutique requesting a "Private Fashion Show for Karen."

Spencer whispered, "Lets finish where we departed earlier. UUUUUUMMMMMMMM, SSSSSSSSSSSSSSHHHHHHHHHHHH," Come down to my office Carmen, so I can show you how attractive I am too you. No, I can't! But, thanks for the invitation. He firmly caressed her arm. He moaned, "SSSSSSSHHHHHHH, could I call you at the boutique?" Sure Spencer! He embraced her extremely firm and said, "It is really nice meeting you." She smiled. It's nice meeting you! She returned to the table getting her purse.

Goodnight Liz! I'm leaving now. You and Melvin have a goodnight. Liz said, "I will see you on Saturday morning." Carmen smiled. "Yes Liz, bright and early!" Carmen walked over to Jessie and Shirley's table, goodnight. Jessie asked, "Are you leaving?" Yes Jessie, I'm getting tired! She stopped by Jackson table before leaving. Goodnight, Jackson and Karen, it was enjoyable seeing you here tonight. Jackson coughed; Carmen, why are you leaving so early? Jackson, I'm awfully tired. He glanced at Karen; excuse me while I escort Carmen out to her car. He kissed Karen; she said, "I will dance with Spencer until you return." He opened the restaurant door; she thanked him. As they walked to her car, she said; "Jackson, I didn't appreciate your behavior at all tonight. Liz mentioned; "Your behavior is becoming extremely dangerous."

He cleared his throat; "Are you attractive to Spencer?" She hesitated before answering him, "What is your damn problem?" Have you forgotten; I'm a single woman? He opened her car door and rubbed his body extremely closely against her. His cock was rock hard. They got into her car. He rested his head against the car seat and declared, "Carmen, Spencer is a bona fide womanizer." She shook her head. Yes Jackson, I know! He shopped at my boutique in the past. He moaned, "Lets go for a ride, so we can talk." She calmly said, "No Jackson! I'm not leaving here with you tonight." He ran his hand through her hair; Carmen, do you remember when we first met? No Jackson, I don't remember! They both were overjoyed with laughter. He caressed her legs; how soon we forget? Yes Jackson, I remember everything from the moment we first met! I had a wonderful time. She assertively said, "I have frequently thought about you for weeks, but then I returned to reality." He seemed irritated. "Carmen, what is reality?" You are married Jackson, and we are definitely "Forbidden Lovers."

He whispered, "Carmen, please kiss me. No Jackson!" She slowly kissed him. "AAAAHHHH," he moaned. Carmen, you know how much I want you tonight. She kissed his cheeks while slowly caressing his neck. She whispered, "Jackson, you've had too much to drink." He asked, "Why does that matter?" She kissed his mouth, "She could taste the alcohol in his mouth, yet he tasted so wonderful." Baby, "Will you suck my cock?" No Jackson! Carmen, "Why do you tell me, "No," when you know you will!" Jackson, you are so positive that you know me – extremely well. He moaned, "My cock is throbbing, EEEEEEEEERRRRRRR. I want to stroke my hard throbbing cock in your pussey." The alcohol was extremely strong on Jackson's breath. He moaned and groaned, "SSSSSSSSSSHHHHHHH," while sliding his ass back and forth on the car seat. He removed his cock; he moaned, "AAAAAAAAHHH, as he stroked his hand faster and faster up and down his cock." He moaned, "Carmen, I'm going to EEEEEERRRRRR. Carmen shit! Baby, I want you so badly." She demanded; "Jackson please stop! You really should stop what you are doing." Damn Carmen! You are no fun tonight! You didn't care that I acted out of control when we first met. She rolled down her car windows. Yes Jackson! But, we know better, and I refuse to continue this type of behavior with you. He zipped his pants, "So what are you really telling me Carmen?" Jackson, I'm serious; I will not continue disrespecting myself with you. As I said earlier, "You possess no shame. Your wife is in the restaurant waiting on you, and you are behaving like an uncontrollable wild animal." He moaned, "GGGGGGGRRRRRRRRR, you bring out my animal instincts." She softly whispered, "Jackson, goodnight. I will see you later!"

She arrived home safety. As she unlocked her door, she said, "Tonight was an incredible "Girl's Night Out." As she stepped from the shower her phone ranged. Hello. Hi Carmen, it's Jessie. Hi Jessie, I recognized your voice. He snapped; "Where the hell did you and Jackson go tonight." She sat on her bed; I don't understand your question Jessie. He said, "The hell you don't know what I'm talking about." They both became extremely quite; Jessie finally spoke; "Damn Carmen! Karen questioned where Jackson had disappeared too, so she ended up sitting at the table with Shirley and me until Jackson returned inside."

She asked, "Where was Shirley's friend?" Damn Carmen! That's beside the point. "Jessie, what is the point?" Carmen, you left with Karen's husband while she sat and waited for his return. "Now, where in the hell did you and Jackson go?" Jessie, we were in my car. Carmen, that isn't true, "I strolled the entire parking lot; you and Jackson were no where to be found." She replied; "Perhaps, you overlooked my car." Carmen, you are making me incredibly angry. Jessie, please calm down. Carmen, "Why don't you take things serious anymore?" Jessie, I have been serious all my life, and now I'm having fun. Well Carmen, being with another woman's husband isn't my idea of having fun. Jessie, please don't lecture me. Carmen, I'm seriously thinking about telling Karen about your affair with Jackson. "Don't you dare Jessie?" He yelled; "Jackson didn't hesitate telling me about you and his affair!"

Jessie, I don't believe you want Shirley knowing about you and me, or should I say, "Valerie Iverson." He repeated, "Valerie Iverson." Yes, that's what I said, Jessie, "Valerie Iverson!" Carmen, what about her?" For starters Jessie! You have called me on many occasions from Valerie's home not to mention the numerous trips; you two have taken together. Carmen, why should Shirley believe you? Jessie, I hired a private investigator to watch you. I found it rather strange; your car was never parked at work when you were claiming to be there. Yes, I have pictures; I have logs with you signing into hotels and most of all; I have video taken with you and Valerie. He asked, "Doing what?" Jessie, you are pretending to be innocent. Go ahead Jessie! Tell Karen, but she loves Jackson enough to forgive him. "Can you say; the same thing about Shirley?" Gosh, Carmen! "Why didn't you tell me sooner?" Jessie, you are no longer important in my life, therefore, I have moved on. Yes, you are terrific in bed, but Sweetie I've had better! Jessie became infuriated; I'm warning you Carmen; you should be extremely careful when dealing with Jackson?

He said, "Lets stop this nonsense. Can, I come over?" Jessie no, that would be awfully disrespectful to Shirley! I wouldn't dream of that and besides, where are you calling from? He whispered, "Look outside your window. I'm parked on your driveway. Please open the door." No Jessie, I will not! He demanded; "If you don't open your damn door, I will kick the son of bitch down." She jumped up and turned on the alarm; go ahead Jessie, and I will call 911. Tonight has been really marvelous, so Jessie please don't spoil my mood. You are right Carmen, I'm really sorry! Goodnight. Goodnight Jessie. Carmen felt slightly nervous but quickly got dressed for bed. She sighed, "Tomorrow, Liz and I will began planning for the "Fashion Show."

Chapter Six

Fashion Show

When Carmen arrived at the boutique, she was surprised that Liz was not already there. "HMMMMMMMMMM," I guess Ms. Carlson is spending this morning with Melvin. As soon she opened the door, Liz drove into the parking lot. Sorry Carmen, I overslept. That's definitely okay. The main thing is – you arrived safely. Liz, you are always punctual, so being late sometimes is okay. "So how was your night with Melvin?" It was great Carmen! Melvin proposed to me last night before leaving Spencer's. She extended her hand, showing her ring. Carmen hugged her and said, "Wow, it's beautiful! What did you tell him?" Carmen, I told him, "Yes!" I'm not getting any younger; plus, I love Melvin more than anything in this world. "UUUUUUUMMM Liz, I can imagine it feels great loving someone that strongly." Yes Carmen, it's the best feeling any women can experience! Yea Liz, I bet! Carmen, you can't imagine what you are missing. Congratulations Liz! Thanks for being concern but one day; I will find out what I'm missing out on but for now, I'm extremely happy.

Liz, do we have any appointments for today? Yes Carmen, Mr. & Mrs. Smith! Carmen responded, "Not Audrey and Keith Smith." Yes Carmen! "Why are you so surprise? Liz, when did they call? They called twenty minutes before closing on yesterday. You marched into the boutique and began talking about the "Fashion Show;" and I forgot to mention their phone call. She's looking for a black leather outfit. As Carmen walked into her office, she said, "Liz please select a number of outfits before Mrs. Smith arrive. There's a black leather dress, and don't forgot the purple pants and jacket. "And yes! The matching shoes for the outfits." Also, Karen Harper would like a purple outfit similar to what I was wearing last night. Okay Carmen, I'll see what I can do for her!

The boutique door opened, Good morning, Mr. & Mrs. Smith. Good Morning; Carmen Sweetie. Can, I get you two a cup of coffee? Sure, Carmen. Mrs. Smith, Liz has chosen a number of leather outfits for you; they are in the fitting room. Carmen, I enjoyed the "Private Show" at my home. You promised to call to schedule another showing, but Keith and I never heard from you. Right Mrs. Smith, Liz and I are planning a "Fashion Show" and decided to wait until then.

Liz walked over; Mrs. Smith, I have placed your outfits in the fitting room. She walked into the fitting room and returned wearing a black leather short shirt and jacket. Keith gasped, "Audrey, don't try on anything else. This is exactly, what we have been looking for." Carmen asked, "Were you two looking around other Shops prior to coming here?" Audrey nervously laughed. "Yes, we did! Mr. & Mrs. Smith always stop here first; you will never be disappointed." Audrey smiled. "That's so true because I have purchased so many lovely outfits from here. She walked in front of the mirror; Keith are you sure; you like this outfit. He kissed her; you look lovely Audrey. Carmen placed her hands into her pockets. Mr. & Mrs. Smith, there are three more outfits in the fitting room. Mr. Smith replied; "No Carmen, this is the outfit; we will purchase!"

Keith walked closely to Carmen as Audrey walked into the fitting room and said, "I convinced Audrey too come here today because I really wanted to I see you." Lets have lunch soon. Okay Keith, what about next Wednesday at noonish? "Where should we meet?" He replied, "What about Spencer?" She shook her head, no, not at Spencer's? Keith, I will call you. She noticed, his cock becoming extremely stiff. He licked his lips and whispered, "Carmen, I can't wait until you sat your hot pussey on my throbbing cock." She thought, "Gosh Audrey, please take your horny husband home." As Carmen rung up the purchase, she asked, "Audrey, do you care to browse around the boutique." Audrey inquired, "What do you think, Keith?" It's up to you, Audrey. "Carmen recommended; why don't you wait until the "Fashion Show?" At the show, you will have an opportunity to model in leather, sequence, cashmere, eveningwear, sleepwear, swimwear and any other special requests from our clientele. I will be contacting each of my clientele by phone, to include, personal invitations requesting RSVP. Sweetie, I look forward to participating. Thanks, Mr. & Mrs. Smith.

Liz, everyone is looking forward to the "Fashion Show." We should compose the guest list to contact everyone really soon. I will begin working on the guest list this upcoming weekend, since Melvin and I are planning to stay home. Also, Melvin has agreed to video record the show. Liz, I have a surprise for you. Liz repeated; "Surprise." Yes Liz! You have been a blessing to Boshae`. Your dedication and devotion has thoroughly played a key role in Boshae` success over the years. Therefore, I solicited Jackson to draw up legal documents giving you thirty-five percent ownership into Boshae`. Once you and Melvin are married, I will have Jackson modify the legal documents adding Melvin's name. Liz, Boshae` truly wouldn't be successful without you and that's a fact. Tears rolled from Liz's eyes; "Carmen, thank you so much!"

The boutique door opened, Randolph and Ruth Jenkins walked in. Ruth was in an awfully cheerful mood. Hello Carmen, Darling! We were in the neighborhood and decided to stop by to browse the boutique. Mrs. Jenkins, we have many new items, which will be exhibit during the "Fashion Show" next month. I would love for you too model. Ruth appeared embarrassed; Darling, I have never modeled in my life. Carmen confidently responded, "Neither has Audrey Smith, Karen Harper, Shirley Wilson, or Liz Carlson." Liz laughed and said, "No Carmen, I'm not modeling!" See Ruth, Liz feels the same way, but she will be out there with the rest of you. They all cheerfully laughed. Carmen glanced at Randolph remembering how she the sprayed cool whip and cherries on his cock. She remembered how energized he became when she dropped the cherries into his mouth. He stared at Carmen as his cock bulged in his pants. He took a deep breath and closed his coat. As Ruth browsed, he whispered to her, "When can I see you again?" Randolph, you will see me at the "Fashion Show." Carmen Sweetheart, I have been thinking about you since the day at the "Cabin." Randolph, that was only yesterday. I know; but damn, it seems longer! Carmen, what are you doing tonight or tomorrow? Randolph, I truly don't have much time right now, but I promise in the future. "How far into the future Carmen?" She didn't answer him.

He moaned, "UUUUUUMMMMMMM, Carmen, I want to eat your cunt. My cock is throbbing. SSSSSSSSHHHHHHHH, I want to feel my cock sliding back and forth in your wet juicy cunt." Ruth returned from the fitting room and responded, "Randolph, you were engrossed in a rather serious conversation with Carmen." Yes Ruth! I'm was getting information about the upcoming "Fashion Show." Ruth hugged Carmen; Darling, I will be expecting an invitation soon.

The next day, Liz and Carmen made preparation for the "Fashion Show." Audrey, Ruth, Shirley, Karen, Nanita`, Valerie, and Liz were selected as models. Two weeks later, the boutique received one hundred and sixty RSVPS. Carmen was extremely excited; Liz, this will be an evening – we will never forget! I will make arrangements for Spencer's Restaurant and Lounge to cater the food for the event, to include, the music and a no host bar. Liz, to add more zest to the show, "I will hire a consultant from Carroll's Facial and Hair Design." Melvin will be recording the show and, of course, Jackson and Jessie will stand around as spectators' of the event.

The day of the "Fashion Show" finally arrived. As the guess mingle, Carmen noticed Jackson and

Jessie shaking hands and chatting momentarily with each other. She took a deep breath; "This is going to be a great show." Ladies and gentlemen please take your seats; we will begin the "Fashion Show" in approximately five minutes. While making that announcement, she almost choked. She was flabbergasted Jackson and Jessie were involved in an intense conservation. She was unsure of their motives, "What are they scheming up? I will find out later, but for now I will host my show." Good evening, thanks everyone for attending. Tonight will be filled with beautiful fashions and lovely models. Underneath your seats, you all will find clipboards and pens to write down any items you might have interest in trying later. Also men feel free to write down items you would love seeing your lady model.

Coming out on the runway is Mrs. Audrey Smith; she's wearing a black belted coatdress made of stretch crepe. It has a thigh-high slit. She's wearing a pair of split vamp pumps. You are looking incredibly lovely Mrs. Smith. Next is Mrs. Nanita` Blanco, she's wearing a blue leather dress and a pair of blue and black sling back shoes. She's also wearing a gold chocker to accessorize her outfit. Thanks Mrs. Blanco, you are looking as striking as ever. Stepping out on the runway is Mrs. Ruth Jenkins. Ladies and gentlemen, Mrs. Jenkins is wearing a purple wool pants suit for you business minded women. She's wearing a pair of black ankle boots. For a night out after work, she's wearing a black sheer sleeveless blouse – Mrs. Blanco removed her jacket. Now, this is a great transformation from business to a night out on the town. Come out on Mrs. Karen Harper. Work it, Mrs. Harper! She's wearing a red evening dress with a slit from her neckline to her panties line. Work-it, Mrs. Harper! This dress is a must for the holiday season, ladies. This dress will sure turn heads. Mrs. Harper is also wearing a pair of red sequence sling back pumps. She's wearing a pearl choker and matching earrings. Thanks, Mrs. Harper! You are simply gracious. Walking out on the runway is Ms. Shirley Wilson. She's wearing a rust tunic dress with splits on both sizes and a matching coat jacket and a printed scarf. She's also wearing a pair of rust pumps. Wow, Ms. Wilson, you look great! Ladies, rust is the perfect winter color, and it is a great color for woman with all shades of complexions not to mention; these coatdresses are the Fall and Winter Fashion Trend for this year. Here's Boshae` co-owner Ms. Liz Carlson. Ms. Carlson is wearing a hunter green mini skirt and black and hunter green printed cashmere sweaters. Too make her outfit look funkier; Ms. Carlson is wearing a pair of med-calf black boots. Ladies, she's carrying a full-length fur coat. She slipped on the fur coat. There were echoes in the audience. Yes, this coat Ms. Carlson is wearing is a must have ladies for this season! Last! We have Ms. Valerie Iverson; she is wearing a pair of black leather pants, and black bikers jacket and a pair of black ankle boots. Eat your hearts out. Ms. Iverson is wearing a gold thong backless bodysuit underneath her jacket to add more sex appeal to her outfit. If there are any Bikers Babes in the audience, this leather suit also comes in red, winter white, purple, and orange. The orange is smashing. Ladies, please take time to try this outfit on.

Now, the fashion show will take a different twist. We have many fashions, but I would like volunteers from the audience to model. There are swimwear, eveningwear, sleepwear, and much more. Ms. Carlson is standing at the rear of the boutique, so volunteers please sign up and please have fun. Right now, we will break for a one-hour intermission. A dinner buffet is catered from Spencer's Restaurant and Lounge along with a no host bar. Enjoy, mingle and again thank you everyone for coming tonight. Ladies, don't forget to sign up in back of the boutique.

Carmen walked in the back of the boutique to briefly talk with Liz. Liz, you were stunning. This turned out better than I could have ever imagined. Hopefully, the women will signup. Liz said, "Carmen, make an announcement – there's only enough time left for three women to model?" Carmen announced; "Can, I get everyone's attention. The modeling portion of the "Fashion Show" will be opened up for an additional thirty minutes after dinner. Liz will signup the first three women, so ladies please hurry in the back of the boutique." Liz raised her hands. Carmen joyfully smiled. "Great, we have three volunteers, thanks!"

Carmen walked up to Jackson and Jessie as they talked. "How are things going with you two – gentlemen?" Jackson hugged her and said, "The show turned out fabulous!" She stared at Jackson – admiring his sex appeal. She glanced at Jessie noticing that he was dressed to the max as usual. "AAAAAAAAHHHH," Carmen thought to herself, "Jackson, Jessie and I would make a delicious sandwich. Jackson would be the white bread, Jessie would be the brown bread, SSSSSSSSSHHHHHH, and I would be the meat filling." Jackson glanced at Carmen and smiled as if he knew what she was envisioning. He winked at her and she winked back. He later said, "Excuse me." Jackson quickly walked over to Carmen and said, "You look tremendously lovely tonight, but I haven't seen you dressed so conservative, since we met. He sighed, "Carmen, are you planning to model anything?" She smiled. "I haven't given any thought to it, Jackson." He whispered, "Come with me Carmen, I want to show you a swimsuit that I would like to see you model." She sighed, "I don't know Jackson. Which one do you have in mind?" He showed her a thong swimsuit.

She shook her head. "You are kidding, Jackson! I will not model this thong swimsuit." Carmen, please take it off the rack and consider modeling it. No Jackson, I can't! He touched her arm. Carmen, I will see you on the runway wearing that swimsuit. Don't count on it, Jackson. His eyes twinkled as he continued looking at her. Carmen, I'm thanking you in advance because I know I will see you on the runway. She passionately asked, "Am I that obvious?"

An hour had passed. Okay Ladies and Gentlemen, we will begin the second half of the "Fashion Show" in another five minutes. We have three volunteers. Liz said, "We're ready?" Coming out on the runway is Mrs. Mildred Rock-Chester. She is wearing a long black evening gown with a belt laced with diamonds and silver. Mrs. Rock-Chester is accessorized with diamond earrings and a diamond necklace. She's also wearing black pumps with a diamond buckle. Mrs. Rock-Chester has already chosen this dress for New Year's Eve. She will surely be the talk of the party. Thank you Mrs. Rocker-Chester! Next, we have Ms. Shannon Seamoore. She's wearing a snake printed leather pants suit with snakeskin pumps. Depending upon the atmosphere, Ms. Seamoore can remove her jacket and catch the crowd attention in this beige sheer backless bodysuit. Ms. Seamoore is wearing this outfit with elegance, and she will definite be a crowd stopper. We have two more models. Liz will host the remaining of the show. Thanks Carmen! Next, we have Mrs. Eliza Romany. She's wearing a black lace teddy with matching black robe. She's wearing a pair of black silk slippers. Now, this is a great way, ladies to relax with your man on a cold winter night. This will surely crank his fire! "There was laughter in the crowd." Ladies and gentlemen, the best is always saved for last. Coming out on the runway is Ms. Carmen Hailey, owner and operator of Boshae` Boutique. Ms. Hailey is wearing a black thong swimsuit with gold embroidery with matching black and gold pumps. Carmen strolled out on the runway moving her body with the music. She walked to the end of the runway smiling at Jackson. He was so thrilled; she was modeling in the swimsuit. She could see the lust in his eyes. Jessie eagerly smiled. Randolph, of course, sat at the end of his chair clapping his hands with excitement. Carmen turned on the runway as she swung her arms from side to side.

Spencer's crew worked in back of the boutique clearing the dishes when a loud sound of breaking dishes echoed. Liz jokingly said, "Ms. Hailey is so stunning until she is breaking dishes in the house tonight." The crowd roared with laughter and clapping! Ms. Hailey, you look absolutely gracious. Carmen took the microphone from Liz. Thanks again, everyone for coming out tonight! If it was not for your business, Boshae` would not be in existence. She thanked each model for participating. You all were total knockouts.

It's time for a big drawing. When everyone entered tonight, they were handed a ticket to write their names on it and turn-in for a drawing. "Have everyone dropped their tickets in the glass dish located at the back of the boutique?" If not, I will give you a few minutes to do so. The drawing is for a leather outfit of your choice. Okay, I need a volunteer from the audience to draw a name. No volunteer. Mr. Harper, "Why don't you come and select a name?" Carmen smiled at Jackson as he walked to the front of the boutique. "UUUUUUUMMMMMMM," he is awfully handsome. He reached into the dish and drew a ticket. Carmen said, "Okay, we have a winner." He handed Carmen the ticket. Carmen read the ticket and said, "I need someone from the audience to read the winner's name." She walked in the audience and handed the ticket to a lady. Mrs. Carlos please read the name appearing on the ticket. The winner is Mrs. Karen Harper. Carmen smiled. "Congratulations! Karen Harper is the winner of the drawing and such luck. Karen Harper is Jackson Harper's wife. Ladies and gentlemen, there are numerous designer outfits to make a selection from. Please have fun while you shop for your favorite items. If I don't have what you are looking for, I will express order. Have fun browsing, but do purchase your favorite items from the show tonight."

Carmen walked over to Liz and said, "I will be back shortly after I change out of this swimsuit." Sure Carmen! She went into her office to change when she heard a knock at the door, Jessie. Hi Baby, I wanted to tell you; how beautiful, you are tonight! "How about next weekend – you, me and that swimsuit?" She responded; I will let you know. He hugged her asking her to wear the, "Snakeskin leather pants suit and snakeskin pumps." Yes Jessie, I will wear that outfit for you! "Will you tell Liz to bring me that outfit?" As soon as, Jessie kissed Carmen another knock echoed the door. Jessie opened the door. Carmen, it's Jackson. Jessie told Jackson to come in as he was leaving. Hi Jackson. Carmen, thank you for modeling the swimsuit. Gosh, you were stunning! He whispered, "Ms. Hailey come over here and give me a kiss." Jackson took her into his arm and kissed her extremely passionately. His cock is rock hard. "UUUUUUUMMMMMM," Carmen my cock is throbbing. OOOOOOHHHHHHHH, she stuck her tongue into his mouth as he groaned, "AAAAAAAAAAAAAHHHHHHHHHHHH."

She heard someone knocking at the door. Jackson opened the door. Carmen, it's Liz. Liz smiled. "I have your change of clothes." Thanks Liz! Liz cleared her throat. Jackson, Karen is looking for you. She wants your opinion on a few outfits. He glanced at Carmen and walked out. Carmen returned in the snakeskin outfit; Jessie walked over and said, "Gosh! Carmen you look so delicious. He moaned, "OOOOOOOOOHHHHHHHH, I will buy this outfit for Shirley." Shirley walked over; Carmen hugged her and thanked her again for modeling. Jessie asked Shirley, "What do you think about the outfit Carmen is wearing." She sighed, "I love it! I want to purchase that outfit, to include, a black evening dress." He asked, "Which one Baby?" The red evening dress, but I want it in a black. He stared at Shirley with a look of excitement on his face.

Carmen rang the night's sales. She thought; "This was the biggest one day sale since opening Boshae`. Gosh! I must thank Randolph Jenkins." She walked over to Randolph; I would like to personally thank you. This is truly the best one day sale, since I began operating Boshae`. He smiled. Carmen, you know how you can show your gratitude. He soundly moaned, "SSSSSSSSSSSSSSSSSSHHHHHH, AAAAAAHHHHH. I would like to share another idea with you." She held both hands together and smiled. If it is anything like this Randolph, I will meet you next week. He quickly asked, "Where? He nosily exhaled, "Back at the cabin!" No Randolph! Lets find another location. Carmen, I will call you. Randolph,

"Give me a clue?" He passionately responded at her, "Cosmetics." Great Randolph!

Carmen said, "Goodnight and thanks everyone." She smiled. "Thank you, all for coming out tonight. I look forward to seeing everyone at Boshae` future events. Please make sure you fill out your evaluation cards prior to leaving. Goodnight everyone." Melvin helped Carmen and Liz cleaned the boutique. Carmen said, "Liz, there were ten fur coats purchased. I don't recall how many leather outfits. We sold every color and size in that thong swimsuit. Liz, this was our best one-day sale, since we opened." Carmen, this was truly a great idea! She hugged Liz and Melvin and said, "Goodnight and please drive safely." Carmen drove home thinking about Jackson and Jessie's behavior. She thought," I still haven't figured out what those two were up too tonight, only time will tell."

Chapter Seven

Dinner for Three

The next morning the phone awakened Carmen. Hello. Hello Carmen. It's Jessie. Hi Jessie. Carmen, were you still asleep? Yes, Jessie, I didn't realize how tired I am! "Are you busy tonight at 6:00 P.M?" No! "Why do you ask?" I would like to take you for dinner tonight. Sure, as long as we don't meet at Spencer's! Carmen, where would you like to go? "Michello` Winery and Eatery on 6th and Pine." Sure, I heard the food is splendid. Okay, I will see you at sixish.

He cleared his throat. Carmen, will you at least have an opened mind tonight during dinner. Jessie, "Why are you making such serious request?" No reason in particular, but will you be opened to new ideas. I want you to experience things; you have never dreamed of. Bye-Jessie. She thought to herself, "Jackson and Jessie are getting weirder each day." Laughing, "But they are both great friends and great fucks." Wonder what it would be like to fuck them both at the same time. She said at the top of your voice, "Oh hell, I will never do that!" She got out of bed and drove to the gym. As she opened the door, the telephone ranged. Hello, Carmen. Jackson, why are you calling me? He hesitated; Baby, I'm calling to see if you have plans for tonight. Yes Jackson, I have plans! "With whom?" Jackson, "Why do you ask?" He sighed, "I'm curious to know, and is it with anyone that I know?" She didn't answer. Carmen are you having dinner with Jessie tonight. And if I am, will this create a problem with you? He whispered, "I would love to be a part of your plans? I know you will enjoy having a threesome with Jessie and me, or perhaps even a foursome." No Jackson, I'm not interested! Have a goodnight, Carmen. Jackson, do you and Karen have plans for tonight? No Carmen, Karen flew to California this morning to assist her sister with her newborn baby. Wonderful, Jackson that will be a nice break for her! Bye-Jackson. Bye-Carmen. Carmen unplugged her phone and took a nap. She awakened at 4:15 P.M. Hell! I should get dressed for my dinner date with Jessie.

Carmen dressed in a black coatdress with a really low cut and a pair of black and gold pumps. She strolled into the restaurant and was escorted to Jessie's table. She discovered someone else sitting at the table with his back turn and thought; "That person surely resembles Jackson from a distance." When she approached the table, "She clearly knew it was Jackson Harper sitting at the table with Jessie." She became angry; I don't believe this, "What the hell are those two up too?" She looked intently at Jessie, "What is Jackson doing here?" Jessie sipped from his drink; I invited him too join us. "Why?" I thought you and I were having dinner alone. Carmen, Jackson called me earlier today and said, "Karen is out of town for one week, and I thought; it would be admirable for you and me to entertain him. I called you, but didn't get an answer. So, I invited him to join us because I didn't think; you would mind. " She continued standing; I unplugged my phone, and I didn't listen to my messages prior to leaving home. Jessie cleared his throat. "I have been told that you can't get enough of Mr. Harper's vanilla lightening rod." She nearly laughed. "Jessie, please stop. I really don't feel Jackson should here tonight." Jackson lustfully smiled. "Come on Carmen, it's only, "Dinner For Three!" Sure Jackson, "Dinner For Three", so after dinner will there be, "Fucking for three." He licked his lips and said, "That can be arranged." Jackson, I'm not in the frame of mind for your dry humor. She abruptly asked, "How to you recommend that you and I entertain Jackson tonight?" Jessie glanced at Jackson and said, "I'm not sure Jackson, but I will let us know after dinner."

She shook her head; Jackson, "You couldn't find anyone else to have dinner with besides Jessie and me? Or, should I say to entertain you." He shrugged his shoulders; Carmen, Jessie invited me. Are you telling to me, I should have declined his invitation? She sat at the table; lets have dinner, so I can get back to the comfort of my home. Something, I haven't take pleasure in for quite some time. The Waitress came to the table, "Can, I get anyone a drink before dinner?" Jackson ordered Scotch, Jessie ordered Gin on the rocks, what about you Miss! Yes, I will have a Club Soda with a twist of lemon. Jackson smiled. "The lady is saying she will have a Martini." I can speak for myself Jackson – the lady is saying, "She will have a Club soda with a twist of lemon!" Okay coming right up.

Jackson asked, "What else did you do today besides working out at the gym?" Nothing more than relaxed which my body really needed. He teased, "Now that, you've had a good work out at the gym; Jessie and I can work you out in other ways." Jackson thanks, but no thanks! Jessie responded, "Are you saying; you can't handle the both of us?" She smiled but didn't respond. No one at the table was saying a great deal. "This was unusually abnormal for the three of them." Jessie broke the ice by saying; "The Fashion Show" was a big success last night! She agreed. Yes, it was! Everyone had an excellent time. Not to mention, Boshae` profit margin for one day was extraordinary. "So what did you think about the swimsuit?" You were beautiful, as I knew you would be. Even though you said, "You wouldn't wear the swimsuit." I knew; I would see you on the runway.

Jessie asked, "How did you two meet?" I met Carmen at the airport. We literally ran into each other. Jessie placed his hand underneath his chin. You ran into each other and it seem, as you two can't stop running into each other. Oh Jessie, what Jackson is saying, "He bumped into me when he was running back to the ticket counter to pick up his wallet; he left behind." So, "How did you two end up fucking each other?" She appeared irritated by his questions. Now, Jessie you are stepping your boundaries. I decline to answer any more of your questions. Now excuse me, she got up from the table. No Carmen, please don't leave! Oh, don't panic, I'm only going to the ladies room.

As she walked to the ladies room, she said hello to man standing alone. Hello Carmen. Great! "Fashion Show" last night! He extended his hand introducing himself as Marco Carlos. Carmen said, "It's a pleasure meeting you Marco." By the way, you really were stunning in that black swimsuit. Thank you Marco! "Who did you escort to the Fashion Show?" Renae`! Oh yes, Renae` Carlos! Right, she mentioned that her husband owns and operates

Michello` Restaurant. Great meeting you Marco! And, I look forward to seeing you and Renea` at future engagements at Boshae`. "You will. Enjoy your dinner, Carmen." She said, "I will try my best."

She returned to the table with Jackson and Jessie. "Did you guys miss me?" Thinking to herself, "I will continue talking dirty to them. She sipped from her club soda." "UUUUUUUUMMMMMMM, this drink taste SOOOOOOOOOOOOOOO GOOOOOOOOOOO. It really feels soothing going down my throat. UUUUUUUMMMM, SSSSSSSSHHHHHHH." She passionately licked the rim of her glass and slid her index finger around the rim of the glass moaning extremely softly. "UUUUUUUUMMMMMMMMMMMMMM, AAAAAAAAAAAAAAAHHHHHHHHHHH, I'm imagining each of your hard throbbing cocks sliding in my hot wet pussey. SSSSSSSHHHHHHH, Jessie and Jackson, I want your stiff cocks right about now." Jackson and Jessie said, "At the same time, we can leave now." She glanced at her watch, "What's taking our dinner so long?" I'm starving. Jessie teased, "Will two stiff cocks satisfy your appetite?" Before she could answer, the Waitress brought their dinners to the table "Can, I get you three anything else?" Yes, a Martini for the lady! Jackson, you are determined to get me drunk hoping; I would end up fucking you and Jessie. Beside, Jessie isn't into kinky sex. Jessie began laughing. "Don't tell me Jessie; you have allowed Jackson to corrupt your mind?" No Carmen, Jackson hasn't corrupted my mind! But, fucking two ladies at once is electrifying. Jessie you are sick; did you force Shirley? Carmen, I didn't force her; it simply happened. "With whom?" Don't answer Jessie, I already know. You fucked Shirley and Valerie Iverson at the same time. Gosh Jessie! Valerie is Pauline's cousin. Carmen, it wasn't planned; it simply happened. "Is that the reason why Valerie stopped seeing you?" She got tired of dealing with your nonsense. Carmen, Valerie and I have difference of opinion in our sex lives. Now, I understand why you have been with Shirley for so long – because she tolerates your bullshit. Thanks for dinner; it was great! The Waiter asked, "Would anyone care for desert or another drink?" Jackson and Jessie ordered another drink. The Waiter asked, "What about you Miss?" She will have another "Martini." Thanks Jessie!

Carmen thought, "I will continue where I left off earlier. UUUUUUUMMMMMM, Jackson and Jessie, my pussey is getting SOOOOOOOOOOO hot and wet from thinking about your cocks. I want to feel your cocks fucking me now. YEEEEEESSS." She whispered, "AAAAAAAHHHHHHHHH. I want you Jessie to fuck my pussey while I suck Jackson's cock." She stuck her finger into her drink and slowly licked the drink from it. "AAAAAAAHHHHHH."

The Waiter returned to the table and said, "Mr. Carlos sent this drink over to the lady." She said to the Waiter, Please thank, "Mr. Carlos for me." Carmen finished her drinks. She glanced at her watch and said, "It's getting late. I want to arrive home to watch television prior to retiring for the night!" Jackson and Jessie both asked, "Alone." Yes! Is there anything wrong with watching television alone?

Jackson caressed Carmen's hand. Why don't you come spend time with Jessie and me tonight?" I rented a room with a Spa, so the three of us could relax together for a while. No Jackson! I'm not Shirley Wilson, therefore; I will not fucking the two of you. Especially, since I know the both of you. Carmen don't be a prude, "If Jessie and I if were total strangers, would you fuck us then?" Not at all! Jessie sighed, "Will you bring the lady another drink?" Carmen raised her hand, no thanks! I've had enough. Well, let's go to the room, and I will order drinks. She agreed, "Sure, why not." Jackson said, "Why don't you and Jessie leave your cars in the parking lot and ride with me?" No Jackson, give me the address! I will meet you there, so I will not be obligated to wait on a ride from either of you. Okay, here's the address! She got up from the table; see you there.

While riding the hotel elevator to room 1206, she thought back too when she and Jackson first met. She knocked on the door; Jackson opened the room. Jazz music was playing in the background. He smiled, "I have ordered drinks." Excellent Jackson! I really want another drink too relax. "Where is Jessie?" He stepped out. She persistently asked, "Where did he go?" Calm down Carmen, he will return shortly. She said, "I don't know why I permitted you to persuade me to come here. He walked over to her, Baby you really turned me on in the restaurant. I wanted to position you on the tabletop and eat your pussey right there in public and didn't care who watched. She moaned, "UUUUUUUUMMMM". She slowly placed her tongue into his mouth but stopped when the door opened. She whispered, "Stop Jackson! That's, Jessie at the door with someone." When he entered the room, she checked to see who was with him. She angrily said, "Shirley." Shirley spoke to Carmen. It's, good seeing you again. Carmen thought to herself, "Not a foursome." Let me get the hell out of this room. I really must leave Jackson. Come on Carmen don't leave, the party has barely started. No Jackson, not with me! I'm going home.

Jackson took her by the arm; Carmen, can I talk with you? She rushed out onto the deck; Jackson start talking and make it good. I don't believe you and Jessie pulled this preposterous stunt. "How dare you and Jessie make these plans; and assume, I would entertain them?" I believe you two have lost your minds. Now, if Jessie and Shirley is into fucking this way, let them go ahead, but don't include me. Carmen, I don't want Shirley, I only want you. Jackson, you are so horny for a threesome until you will fuck Shirley without thinking twice. Jackson, I can't continue agreeing to participate in you and Jessie's sick-minded fantasies. Carmen, please calm down and go back inside the room and finish your drink!

Jessie walked out on the deck and said, "He was leaving." Carmen walked back inside the room. Jessie and Jackson stayed out on the deck talking. They returned inside. He said good-bye to Carmen and asked Shirley, "Are you ready to leave?" They said, "Goodnight" and left. Jackson, I hope Jessie didn't tell Shirley; we were planning to engage in a foursome. I don't believe the bullshit you and Jessie tried here tonight. Are you two only concerned with satisfying your sexual fantasies? I have my business to operate and there is no way; I will lose my reputation in town under no circumstances. No Carmen! Jessie told Shirley; he wanted to stop by to visit friends. Jackson, you are married! "How does it look with you entertaining another woman? Everyone in town is aware that you and Karen are married. So, I don't understand; how you can jeopardize your marriage from uncontrolled lust? Damn Jackson! You are an extremely prominent attorney – for Pete sake, think with your intelligence and not your cock. He walked over to her slowly kissing her lips. "Don't be angry.

Jessie and I thought you would be receptive to having a foursome." Damn Carmen – I'm sorry! Shirley will not tell anyone about you being here tonight. She sighed, "Jackson, please swear to me; you and Jessie will never do this bullshit again. I will call Shirley tomorrow and explain why; I was here tonight!" He caressed her back and kissed her neck. She wanted to tell Jackson, "No" but she was too horny to give a damn! She and Jackson kissed and held each other extraordinarily tight. Jackson delightfully pressed his body against her body. He moaned, "UUUUUUUUUUMMMMMMMMMM, Baby." He touched her face with pure fascination. He whispered to her, "I will do anything to satisfy you; whether, it's a threesome or foursome." Baby, I want to please your sexual need. "OOOOOOOOOOOOOOHHHHHHHHH, SSSSSSSSSSSSSSSSSSHHHHHHHHHHH," Baby loosen up, you can have the best time of your life if only you would loosen up. He moaned, "EEEEEEEEEERRRRR, SSSSSSHHHHHHH, my cock is SOOOOOOOOOO hard." He walked her over to the bed. He slowly removed her clothing. "AAAAAAAAAHHHHHHHHHHHHHH, I want to fuck you Carmen, but first I want to taste your pussey." Jackson, your mouth feels, "SOOOOOOO HOOOOOOT." She screamed, "Jackson, please fuck me with your cock; I don't want to wait." As he fucked her, she felt another cock caressing against her lips. She glanced up and there stood Jessie totally nude with his cock against her lips. She slowly opened her mouth and took his cock into her mouth as Jackson fucked her pussey. Jessie was moaning, "AAAAAAAAAAAHHHHHHHHHHHH, Carmen, your mouth feels so awesome sucking my cock." Jackson stopped fucking Carmen to trade positions with Jessie. Jessie began fucking Carmen's pussey with his hard throbbing cock. "OOOOOOOHHHHHHH, Jessie your cock is SOOOOOOOOOOOOOOOOOOOOOOO GOOOOOOOOOOOOOOOOD."

Jackson placed his cock in Carmen mouth while she began bobbing her head back and forth on his cock. Jackson's cock was, "SOOOOOOOOOO hard." She could feel it throbbing in her mouth. "AAAAAAAAAAAHHHHHHHHHHHH," Jackson whispered, "Carmen, Baby suck my cock, don't stop, suck my cock. SSSSSHHHHHHHHH, Baby, suck my cock until I come." Jessie stopped fucking Carmen and laid on his back as she sat her hot wet pussey on his cock. I want you to ride my cock. She relaxingly sat her pussey on Jessie's cock while Jackson slowly slid his cock back and forth in her ass. Carmen couldn't believe how horny she was. AAAAAAAAAAAAAAHHHHHHH, Carmen screamed, "JAAAAACCCCCCCKKSOON both of you fuck me, fuck me until I CUUUUUUUUMMMMMMMMMMMMM. AAAAAAAAAAAAAHHHHHHHHHHHH, Jessie your cock is SOOOOOOOOOOOOOOO GOOOOOOOOOOOOOOOOOOOOOD. AAAAAAAAAAAAAAAAAAAAAHHHHH." Jackson caressed her tits so forcefully. OOOOOOOOOOHHHHHHHHHHHH, she moaned, "SSSSSSSSSSSSSSSSSSHHHHHHH, EEEEEEEEERRRRRRR. Jessie fuck my hot pussey. OOOOOOHHHHHHHHHHHHHHHHH, AAAAAAAAAAHHHHHHHHHHHHHH. Fuck me." Jackson began fucking Carmen's ass faster and faster. Jackson screamed, "OOOOOOHHHH, Carmen, I'm CUUUUUMMMIIIINNNGG, AAAAAAHHHHHHHHHHHHHHHH, I'm CUUUUMMMMMMMMIIIIINNNGGG." Jessie screamed, "AAAAAAAHHHHHHHH, Carmen, please take all of my CUUUUUUMMMMMMMM into your wet and hot PUSSSSSSSSSEEEEEEEEEEEYYYYYYYY. OOOOOOOOOOOHHHHHHHHHHHH, Baby." Carmen screamed, "AAAAAAHHH" as she CAMMMMMMMMMMMED over Jessie's cock." The room was filled with, "AAAAAAHHHHHH, OOOOOHHH, and SSSSSHHHHHHHHHH." The three of them could have recorded "The Sound of

Fucking CD. AAAAAAHHHHHHHH, the three of them were so excited."

Jackson rolled over in bed while Carmen rested her head on his chest. She whispered, "I need to shower, so I can drive home." She got out of bed and went into the bathroom and started the shower. She stepped into the shower. Jackson stepped in minutes later. He kissed her. Carmen, I never thought I would fulfill my sexual fantasies with you. "AAAAAAAHHHHHH," Baby, thank you so much! Thank you for finally participating in a threesome with me." He removed the soap and began lathering her body. He moaned, "OOOOHHHH. UUUUUUUUUUUUMMMMMMMMMMM, your body feels so great." Jackson cock began getting hard again, but he continued lathering her body.

Carmen took the soap and lathered Jackson's body as she kissed his lips. Jessie stepped into the shower. Jackson lathered Carmen in front while Jessie took the soap and lathered her from the back; she was so excited until she could barely stand it. Jessie slowly wrapped his arms around her body and softly rested his head against the back of Carmen's head. Jackson firmly wrapped his arm around Carmen's body and softly rested his head on her forehead as she securely wrapped her arm around Jackson. They all stood in the shower embracing each other. The warm water felt, "SOOOOOOOOOOO good" pounding against their bodies. "UUUUUUUMMMMMMMM," Carmen whispered, "The two of you feel so terrific."

"SSSSSSSHHHHHHHHHHHH," I can stay sandwiched between you two forever. She could feel both Jackson and Jessie cock getting hard. She began moving her ass around and around against Jessie's cock while Jackson began breathing extremely loud. Jessie pressed his cock firmly against her ass. AAAAAAAAAHHH, she could feel her nipples getting so hard until they were aching from the excitement pressing against Jackson check. OOOOOOOOOOHHHHHHHHHHH, Jessie, "AAAAAAAAAAAAHHHHHHHHH, Jackson, UUUUUUUUUUUUUMMMMMMMMMMM." The phone ranged. She moaned, "Gosh Jackson! You should answer the phone. Who knows, you are here?" Jessie said, "No one but Shirley!" They all went into the bedroom dripping with water. Hello. Hi Shirley. Jessie shook his head; tell her I'm not here. No Shirley! I haven't seen Jessie, since he left here with you earlier. If he stops by, I will tell him; you are looking for him. Bye.

Carmen said, "Guys, we should leave now before we cause serious problems." Jessie said, "No! Lets finish fucking." No, I'm getting dress and driving home! If you want to fuck Jessie, "Why don't you fuck Jackson or invite Shirley over, but I'm going home!" Carmen got dressed and drove home. She thought as he stepped from her car, "I never imagined fucking Jackson and Jessie together in a million years. This will never happen again. The nerve of Jessie inviting Shirley over for a foursome! Hell! They have lost their damn minds? "

She walked into the kitchen making a cup of tea when the doorbell ranged. Now, she thought, "Who is at my door." She checked her monitor to see who was at the door. She sighed, "Its Jessie and I can imagine Jackson isn't far behind." She spoke through the intercom. Yes, who's there! Hi Baby, it's Jessie. Jessie, "What are you doing here? Have you forgotten Shirley is looking for you?" I know Baby, but she doesn't know that I'm here. "Can I come in?" Jessie, "No," it's getting really late! Please Carmen, I need to see you; I want to embrace you in my arms. No Jessie, not tonight! I have to get up early in the morning. "Have you forgotten; I operate a boutique?" Please Carmen open the door. No Jessie! Damn Carmen, if I were Jackson knocking on your door you would open the door for that son of a bitch. I watched how you fucked him tonight. You were extra passionate with. You fucked that no good son of a bitch as if he's gift to women. I watched how you kissed that bastard and how you held him in your arms! For Pete sake, Carmen, he's – caucasian. What the hell are you thinking! I expected more compassion from you than what you displayed to me. She was extremely annoyed by his behavior. "Jessie, I knew having a threesome with you and Jackson would create this problem; I was no more passionate with Jackson then; I was with you." He yelled, "Sure you were, Carmen!" Jessie, you've had too much to drink, and you should go home before you find yourself in jail.

No Carmen! I'm pissed at everything that happened tonight. "Now, who fault is that? You co-hearse this nonsense with Jackson, and it backfired on your ass." Jessie yelled, "Carmen open this damn door before I kick the son of a bitch down." My alarm is on so don't be stupid tonight. Carmen, I don't give a damn about the cops. Jessie, "What is wrong with you? And, "Why did you bring Shirley back to that hotel room? Have you lost your mind?" I'm trying my best to be patient with you and Jackson; but I'm getting to the edge of my ropes. Jessie, "What make you assume; you can stop by my home and dictate what goes on in here?" You are not welcome in my home at your discretion. Carmen, open this damn door. He began banging on the door louder and louder. Jessie, you are going to awakened the neighbors. He yelled, "Fuck your neighbors, I don't give a fuck about them." Jessie, go home. Goodnight!

He continued knocking on her door. Jessie, you have five minutes to leave my property, or I'm calling the cops. He yelled, "Go ahead Carmen and you will be sorry." Carmen turned off the intercom, lights and walked upstairs to get ready for bed. Minutes later she heard Jessie driving away. She said, "I really want to get away from this madness. Liz has thirty-five percent ownership into Boshae`; she's doing such a wonderful job operating the boutique during my absence. She sighed; "I will contact my Travel Agency on tomorrow morning, but first, I will discuss my plans with Liz."

Chapter Eight

Seeking Peace of Mind

Carmen was so upset about how she conducted herself during dinner with Jackson and Jessie until she wasn't able to sleep. She decided to shower, dress, and drive over to the boutique. When she entered the boutique it was 4:45 A.M. She sat in her office and thought, "I don't believe my life is beginning to crumble right before my very own eyes. I really must do something quickly; otherwise, Karen and Shirley will end up getting hurt from this bullshit being created by their men. How the hell did I get myself caught in the middle of all this bullshit? Gosh! How did I allow this to happen? Everything is going so great at Boshae`, but one weekend of only being concern for fulfilling my desires will undoubtedly hurt many people. She rested her head against her hands; I'm getting really scared. I have never in the past seen Jessie behave with so angrily. What will he do?"

At 7:00 A.M., the phone ranged. She thought, "Who could be calling here so early?" No one knows; I'm here at the boutique. She thought, "Should, I answer the phone?" She picked up the phone. Hello. There was no response. She thought, "Now what?" She hung up the phone and it ranged again. Hello, this is Carmen. It's Jessie. I'm calling to apologize for my awful behavior last night. She didn't respond. "He was the last person; she wanted to talk with." Carmen are you still here? Yes Jessie, I'm here! But, I can't talk right now. Why, is Jack there with you? No Jessie! Jackson isn't here with me. "So why can't you talk with me?" Jessie, I have a lot on my mind.

I'm extremely disheartened about what transpired last night. You knew prior to inviting me to dinner those were the plans. Please Carmen, hear me out! I want to apologize for inviting Jack to join us for dinner last night. I called him, and discovered that Karen was out of town, so I invited him to join us for dinner. I remembered, you telling me how eager Jack desired a threesome, so I asked him, "Did, he want to fulfill his wildest dream?" She began crying, I noticed Jessie; you were leading the conversation. Jackson knew how I felt about threesomes, so I couldn't figure out why he propositioned a threesome with you. Particularly, since I'm totally against that. "Why did you bring Shirley?" Only because, "Shirley doesn't mind participating in threesomes." Jessie, how could you persuade Shirley into having sex with you and Pauline's cousin? I talked with Valerie months ago and she said, "You invited her to your home and the entire night was really strange after arriving there. She remembered drinking a cocktail and becoming enormously horny. The next thing she knew, the three of you were fucking." Jessie what did you give Valerie to sexually arouse her enough to fuck her cousin's husband. Carmen, "Why in the hell are you trying to act so innocent when you are fucking a married man yourself?" But Jessie, Jackson, never tricked me into fucking him. I choose to fuck Jackson and that's the difference. Valerie fucked you and Shirley against her free will. She didn't have any choice, and she was terribly angry it happened. Jessie, you still haven't answered, "Why did you escorted Shirley to the hotel last night?" I thought, "A foursome would be nourishing for us." Jessie, you are making me sick. I really must go! Carmen, you are acting as if Jackson is a damn saint. No! Jackson is by far from being a saint. I also plan to have a few choice words with him. I'm telling Jackson; the same thing that I have told you. I never want to see you again Jessie, and she hung up the phone!

The phone ranged again, but she didn't answer. "The first time in years she felt so venerable. She has always felt so in control of any situation, but this morning she felt so powerless and frighten." She cried out aloud, "I hate you both, Jackson and Jessie! And, I never want to see either of you again." Carmen walked from her office with her makeup smeared all over her face. Liz entered the boutique; Carmen are you okay? Yes Liz, I'm okay! I don't believe the mess; I have gotten myself into. Lets talk Carmen. No Liz! I'm not in the mood for talking. Liz voice was moderately stern, "Yes, Carmen now!" Liz, I have been having an affair with Jackson Harper. Carmen, I don't believe; you've been having an affair with Karen Harper's husband. How dare, you sleep with her husband and later go to her home for a "Private Fashion Show!" Carmen cried, "Liz, I'm so sorry!" Well Carmen, I suspected; you have been dating Jessie. But, never in a million years would I have suspected; you are having a "Forbidden Love Affair" with Jackson. " When did you get involved with Jackson?" About ten months ago, when I flew to Colorado Springs.

Last night, Jessie invited me to dinner and he, of course, invited Jackson. "Why did Jessie invite Jackson to join the two of you for dinner?" Liz, we ended up having a threesome. Carmen, "Have you lost your damn mind?" No Liz! Please don't make it sound so horrible. Liz screamed, "You have told me on numerous occasions that you wouldn't participate in threesomes under no circumstances. Now, why the hell a threesome with those two?" Liz, I was tricked. Carmen, why are you crying? Jessie stopped by home last night, but I didn't open the door for him. He yelled and screamed, "Accusing me of being more passionate with Jackson." He banged and kicked on my door until I threaten to call the cops. "Did you?" No! He finally drove off, but he called here 7:00 A.M. this morning. "How did he know; you were here so early?" I don't know Liz, but I have gotten myself into a horrible mess. He is threatening to tell Karen about my affair with Jackson. But Carmen, "What about Shirley?" Liz, Jessie escorted Shirley to the hotel room last night. Liz shook her head; does this mean you had a foursome with Shirley, Jessie, and Jackson?" Hell no, Liz! Well Carmen, "Don't worry about Shirley. Did you know she had an affair with Matthew Jones? No Liz! I didn't know.

"Isn't Mathew Jones the husband of Carroll Jones, owner and operator of Carroll Facial and Hair Design?" Liz said, "Call, Shirley right now and tell her to keep her damn mouth shout, or you will reveal her secret to Jessie and Carroll about her affair with Matthew." Liz, why didn't you tell me prior to me asking Shirley to model in the "Fashion Show?" Call, Shirley before Jessie manipulates her into telling Karen about your "Forbidden lover affair" with Jackson. No Liz! I can't do that. You either call Shirley or ruin Jackson' s marriage. Oh, no Liz! I can't ruin Jackson's marriage. "Then, call Shirley now." Okay Liz, what is Shirley's home telephone number?

Hello Shirley, this is Carmen Hailey. Shirley didn't respond. Shirley are you still here? "Why did you come to the hotel room last night with Jessie? Shirley sighed, "Jessie told me someone; he knew was at a hotel room interested in a foursome but had changed their mind when I entered the room. "No Shirley, that's not true!" He said, "You asked he and Jackson out for dinner and proposed having a foursome." Gosh! How could Jessie do that? Jessie called me and said; "His friend had rented a hotel room and wanted him to find a fourth person willing to participate in a threesome." Jessie and I had an intense discussion in the car, and he stated that you only have sex with three or more people at a time. He tried convincing me that you are not as innocent as you portray yourself. I understand Carmen; you have been fucking Jessie and Jackson both for months. He said, "You wanted to escalate your relationship into a foursome, and he mentioned my name." She sighed, "You thought I would be perfect."

No, that's not true Shirley! Shirley, let me tell you one thing, "I don't know what you and Jessie are up too, but I've had enough of your man's nonsense. Talk with him today and tell him that I will not tolerate him slandering my name. Yes! I have fucked him, but I have never implied to him that I'm interested in a threesome or foursome. The nerve of Jessie, "Why is he so anger? Could, it be that he has finally realized that I'm no longer interested in him." Jessie thinks; he and I should reveal your affair to Karen. Shirley, if you discuss this nonsense with Karen, I will indeed reveal your affair with Mathew Jones to Carroll and Jessie. "What are you talking about Carmen?" Shirley, you know exactly what I'm talking about? If I go down, bitch, you go down also. You make the choice whether you stand or fall, but make a wise decision because you will loose and so will Jessie. You are portraying to be so innocent and believing everything Jessie is telling you. But Girlie, there are secrets about you; Jessie Hopkins is unaware of. I don't mind sharing this information with him. "How did you find out about this?" Shirley, it doesn't matter. Carmen, you are simply making this shit up to scare me. Shirley, be aware that I have my resources, and one more thing, "I have a video with you and Matthew fucking each other!" Shirley screamed, "That's a damn lie, Carmen." Shirley, you can take a gamble on this, but bitch, you better have a poker hand. Liz wrote down on a piece of paper, tell her that she was wearing a black and white sleeveless dress and a pair of black vamp pumps. She had a red teddy and a bottle of champagne in her overnight bag. Carmen stated the information written on the paper. Shirley began crying. Carmen asked, "Shirley, did I strike your nerves?" Carmen, please promise me; you won't share this information with Jessie or Carroll, and I promise; I won't tell Karen about your affair with Jackson. Carmen said, "Good-bye."

Liz gave Carmen a high five – great job! You don't have to worry about this information going anywhere. Thanks Liz! Liz, I need a break; I'm leaving town for a couple of months to regain my "Peace of mind" from all of this nonsense; I have created in my life. Carmen, where are you planning to go? I don't know Liz, but I really need to get away. Liz, I don't want anyone knowing where I am other than you for business emergencies. Liz please promise me; you will not reveal this information to anyone. "No matter how persistence Jackson is – under no circumstances reveal my plans to him!"

Liz, I'm going down to visit my Travel Agency as soon as their office opens. Carmen whatever plans you need to make, go ahead, and take as long as you need. Thanks Liz! Carmen eyes became extremely teary. "I promise once I get myself out of this mess; I vow with my total being – this will never happen again as long as I live." Liz, I really hate Jessie. He told Shirley many lies about me as they drove home from the hotel last night. I can only imagine; he told those lies to detract the attention away from himself. Carmen, I told you many years ago to be extremely careful of Jessie. You remember Pauline and I were friends. She revealed many of Jessie's sexual secrets. Yes Liz! You warned me, but of course, I ignored you.

Liz thanks for listening. Gosh Carmen! We are sister and sisters' stick together through thick and thin. Even though we are not birth sister, we're definitely blood sisters. Liz talked with sincerity, "Remember, when we were twelve years old; we stuck needles in our index finger, and touched our bloody fingers together and vowed to be blood sisters for life. We are blood sisters, and I will do any thing to protect you. Carmen, I know you will do the same for me."

Liz sighed, "Why don't you call Jackson to inform him of your plans to leave town?" Liz, this is none of Jackson's business. Okay, you are right. Oh before I forget, Melvin and I have set a wedding date for June 16th. Carmen hugged Liz. Sweetie, that's great! I would like to help with your wedding plans when I will return in late January. Carmen, you really should be here during the holidays. Liz, I need to find the inner peace; I have lost in my life. Being here this holiday won't mean anything to me if everyone else is feeling hurt from this mess. She hugged Liz; I'm leaving for an hour to meet with my Travel Agent. Liz, please don't mention my whereabouts to anyone. "Not even Jackson Harper."

Carmen arrived at the Travel Agency unsure of her travel destination. She talked candidly to the Agent about her potential travel plans. She clutched her purse; the intent of my travel is mainly for sightseeing, relaxing, and primarily having time to create a new vision for my boutique. The Agent listened intensely and then gave her a few brochures. "Ms. Hailey, I know you will enjoy visiting one of these locations." As Carmen glanced towards the doors, Jackson entered through doors. He briefly talked with the receptionist and walked into the office where Carmen was located. Carmen stood; Jackson, what are you doing here? I called the boutique, and I had to drag this information from Liz. She told me you were here making travel arrangements. Gosh Jackson! Liz promised me, she wouldn't tell you under no circumstances that I'm planning to leave town. Liz is extremely worried about you. She thinks; you are being irrational. Baby, the holidays are approaching. He touched her arms, "Why are you running away?" Jackson, I really need time for myself.

He sighed, "Let me make travel arrangements for us. We can leave tonight." No Jackson! Jessie will figure out our little secret, and we will be back to square zero. I've had enough drama to last me a lifetime, and you can rest assure that I'm not leaving town with you. Carmen, I'm sorry things happened the way they did. But, you are also partly the blame because you allowed these things to happen. Carmen, please forgive me for everything. He sighed, "I promise; I will change my behavior." No Jackson! Carmen, I know you will change your mind. Not this time, Jackson. Carmen asked, "Please escort the gentleman to the door." Jackson appeared totally surprised as if he couldn't believe; she really meant, "No!" He knew he could easily persuade her into doing anything he requested of her. But this time, his charm wasn't working. He whispered prior to leaving, "You are mine and don't ever forget." She kept her eyes on him until he walked out the doors. Thank you for asking him to leave. "Ms. Hailey, these are the brochures. Please review them and give me a call once you have decided on your destination." Okay, I will call you on Tuesday!

Carmen stormed into the boutique. "Liz, how dare you tell Jackson about my potential travel plans!" Carmen, Jackson, was really persistence. Damn! So was I. Didn't I ask you not to reveal this information to Jackson? Liz, I thought we were blood sisters and that we would protect each other. Carmen yelled, "Liz don't make me hate you. I have loved you most of my life, but my feelings can change without a moments notice. So, I suggest that you rethink your dedication to Mr. Jackson Harper." I'm sorry Liz; I know how persistence Jackson can be when he wants something really badly. He will stay on your back until he conquer whatever he's in pursuit of. I have given into him on many occasions, but not this time; his charm didn't work. I could see the hurt in his eyes but, "Frankly, I didn't give a damn." His attorney persuasion didn't work in my court of law. They both enthusiastically laughed.

Liz, I'm going home, do we have anyone scheduled for today? Yes, Mrs. Carlos for a New Year's Eve dress and Mr. Jenkins for a fur coat. Mr. Smith and Mr. Blanco came in this morning and purchased fur coats for their wives' for Christmas. Now Liz, "How many fur coats can their wives' owned." There's something definitely bizarre happening with those two. Before, long Mrs. Smith and Mrs. Blanco will have more fur coats in their closets than; we have here at Boshae`. Carmen guess who called this morning. "Who?" Liz smiled. Spencer. He wants you to call him. Liz, did he leave a message? No! But, he can be reached at his restaurant. Okay Liz, I will stop by his restaurant for lunch, and I will call you later from home.

Carmen arrived home and quickly showered. She immediately drove to Spencer's for lunch. Ring. Hello. Liz, this is Carmen, I'm in route to Spencer's for lunch. If you need to get in contact with me, please call me on my cell phone or on Spencer's direct line. "Liz, how did the appointments go?" Mrs. Blanco purchased two dresses. Carmen responded without thinking, "But we only have one New Year's Eve." Carmen don't question why people spend their money at your boutique just be thankful that they do. Without them patronizing the boutique, you wouldn't be as successful as you are today. I guess you are right Liz. Did Mr. Jenkins purchase a fur coat? Yes and a black leather suit! "What style?" Liz laughed. "Like the one, Mrs. Jenkins's purchased during the, Fashion Show." Carmen sighed, "Why does she want two of the same color and style?" Carmen, there you go again – questioning why folk's are spending money at your boutique. They both zealously laughed. Liz continued laughing. "Carmen, you are so funny." Oh Carmen, Mr. Jenkins asked about you. He wants you to call him at his office when you get time. "Liz, did he say why?" No Carmen! But, I'm willing to guess. Oh Liz, don't start assuming. Carmen, it's not an assumption. He wants to taste your brown sugar. Carmen changed the subject. Liz, I will stop by the boutique prior to you close this evening. Bye-Liz.

When Carmen walked into Spencer's, Spencer was standing by the bar talking to his Waitress. He immediately walked over and hugged her exceptionally tight. He whispered, "I didn't expect to see you here today." I decided to stop by for lunch and beside Liz told me; you called earlier. Yes Carmen, I did! "Spencer, for what reason?" I called to invite you to join me on vacation in the Virgin Islands. She slightly placed her hand over her mouth to disguise her smile. Spencer, who will operate your business while you are away? He smiled. Oh, I have a business partner to operate my restaurant during my absence. My brother and I have been operating my restaurant together for five years. Really, I thought you were the sole owner of your restaurant. Carmen, I have operated Spencer solely for ten years, but five years ago; I awarded thirty percent ownership of my business to my brother, Andrea. Andrea is well known in the community, and he will have no problems keeping the business afloat while I'm away.

He rested his head against his hand. I really need a break from this restaurant. Carmen; you would be the perfect person to vacation with. Spencer, do you need an answer tonight? No Baby, at least by Friday! "What about your family?" I'm a single man looking for a wife. She thought, "Why the hell is he telling me this?" She slightly smiled. I will let you know by Friday." She handed him her home phone number and said, "Please call me later tonight." He smiled, "Would you perceive me as being too pushy if I asked for your answer right now?" She shook her head. Sure Spencer, I will join you! Great, I will make reservations later this evening! She held her hands together. Earlier this morning, I visited my Travel Agency but was indecisive about where I wanted to travel. Tears rolled from her eyes. Gosh Spencer! "I really need time away from all the madness; I have created in my life. I was planning to take this trip alone, but it would be great traveling with a companion." He guaranteed her; a vacation would be great for the both of us!

"UUUUUUUMMMMMMMMMMMM," Carmen. We will have SOOOOOOOOOOO much fun. He stared into her eyes. Do you care to share whatever madness; you have created in your life? She shook her head. No Spencer, perhaps some other time! Okay, I'm a patient man. Whenever you feel like talking, I'm available to listen. Please don't keep secrets from me. She glanced at her watch. Spencer as much fun as I'm having, I must leave! He walked her too her car. Carmen, I will call you later tonight. Drive safely.

When she arrived at the boutique, five women were shopping. Hi Liz. Carmen, you are happy. "What sparked this mood shift?" You wouldn't believe Liz, but when I stopped by Spencer's for lunch; he invited me to fly to the Virgin Islands with him for two weeks. Liz squeezed Carmen's arm. I sure hope you told him, Yes, "You are surely to have a wonderful Holiday Season with him!" Oh Liz, I always have a fabulous Holiday Season. By the way, I told Spencer, "Yes!" Will you two have separate rooms? "Liz, not on your life." Carmen, "What will I do with you?" Please continue being my blood sister. Carmen hugged Liz and said, "Thank you, sister for everything!"

Carmen whispered, "Look who's walking in." Liz asked, "Who?" It's Shirley Wilson. Carmen, keep your cool. She's really nice, once, you get to know her. Hi, Ms. Wilson! Can I help you find something? Carmen, I'm here to apologize for everything that has happened over the past two months. Carmen, Jessie and I have ended our relationship after I refused to tell Karen about your affair with Jackson. Jessie and I had been together for six years; and we are ending our relationship over this nonsense. I knew this would happen sooner or later. Shirley, please come into my office. "Can I get you a cup of coffee or tea?" No thanks! Jessie would eventually do the same thing to me as he did to Pauline. I had an affair with Jessie when Pauline was alive and to make matters worse, Jessie and I slept with Pauline's cousin. I should have known better. Shirley began crying out of control. Carmen, Jessie has lied so often to me. He promised to marry me but whenever the date arrived; he has always made excuses to why it wasn't the right time to marry. I stayed with him this long because I thought one day; he would truly marry me. I thought, I loved Jessie, but I know I was fulfilling Pauline's dream. Pauline thought, 'I would be a good match for him but after the lies and cheating, I began seeing other men. She sighed, "Yes, I had an affair with Matthew Jones, and I also tried seducing Melvin, but he truly loved Liz." I have, since apologized to Liz. I didn't know at the time Melvin was seeing Liz. Shirley, I have known this for a while.

Carmen, I refuse to continue living Pauline's dream. Jessie lies and deceit have caused me to despise him. He walks around behaving as if his damn cock is made of precious jewels. Hell! Not to mention, he thinks he's irresistible. He has hurt numerous women with his conceitness. I have always warned Jessie that his games would one day come to an end! Shirley, Jessie mentioned to Jackson and me that you enjoyed having threesome. He said, "You introduced him to Valerie." Damn Carmen, Jessie is being vindictive. He has always been inquisitive about us sleeping with other women or couples. Carmen, I will be honest with you; I hate Jessie and I never want to see him again. Carmen, I must admit; he was awesome in bed. Jessie lied to me for years about him burying himself in his work when in fact he was burying his cock into other women's hot pussies. Jessie has decided to date younger women because he's sick of women our ages. Well Shirley, he's free to make those choices, but hopefully, those young women don't fuck his old ass into unconsciousness.

Shirley, I have a friend; I would like to introduce you too. My friend, Jason Carmichael has asked about you, years ago. He would be the perfect match for you. Carmen, if he's so perfect, "Why don't you keep him for yourself?" Shirley, "He's like my brother to me. When I first met Jason, his primary topic of conversation was his ex-wife." He has long gotten over her, but said, "He's having a difficult time meeting single women." I don't know if he's seeing anyone now, but I could call him to find out. Shirley enthusiastically shook her head. Carmen that would be great if you called Jason! Hello Jason, This is Carmen Hailey. How are thing with you Jason? She hesitated; guess who is sitting in my office?" No Carmen, I can't guess! Shirley Wilson. Yes, Jessie Hopkins' lady friend! Yes! They were together for six years, but they are no longer together. I'm calling too see if you are seeing anyone? Sure Jason, I will give her your home number. Good-bye Jason. Carmen smiled. Jason will call you tonight and please don't discuss Jessie with him. Men find it extremely boring when women discuss their ex-lovers. A man doesn't want to feel that he has to compete with an ex-stiff cock. Shirley bashfully laughed. "Carmen, I'm serious, the hell with Jessie Hopkins." She hugged Shirley, this is Jason's home number – please give him a call. Thanks for stopping by. Good-bye.

Liz walked into the office; why did Shirley visit you? She wanted to discuss Jessie Hopkins. She and Jessie have ended their relationship. Well Liz, he's history. Do you remember Jason Carmichael? Liz smiled. Vaguely! Well, I called him today, and he's not seeing anyone, so I'm playing Ms. Matchmaker. He and Shirley exchanged telephone numbers. Great Carmen! Shirley and Jason will make a great couple;

he's been interested in her for many years. Liz glanced at her watch. I must leave on time tonight; Melvin is cooking dinner for me tonight. Sure Liz, have a terrific dinner with Melvin! Drive carefully Liz. Okay Carmen, you too!

When Carmen arrived home, she decided to call Spencer but as she reached for the phone, it ranged. Hello. Hi Carmen, it's Spencer. I hope; this isn't bad timing. No, this is a great timing! I was in the process of calling when the phone ranged. Carmen, I have made reservation for December 7th through December 29th to the Virgin Islands. I must return in time for the big New Year's Eve Bash here at the restaurant. Ok Spencer, I'm looking forward to this trip. "Carmen, will you stop by for dinner on Tuesday?" Spencer, "What about Saturday? Gosh Carmen! That will seem like an eternity!" Okay Spencer, I will stop by on Tuesday. After she hung up the phone she thought; "I'm finally regaining my, Peace of mind."

Chapter Nine

Twenty-Three Days of Sheer Pleasure

Spencer arrived at Carmen's home on December 7th feeling extremely excited about the "Twenty-Three Days of Sheer Pleasure;" he would be experiencing with her during their vacation. He greeted her with excitement. Good morning Carmen, I want to thank you very much for joining me! She smiled. It's my pleasure and thank you very much for inviting me. He carried her luggage to the car. As he they drove to the airport, he asked, "What made you change your mind about joining me?" She smiled. OOOOOOHHHH, your personality enticed me.

Their flight arrived safely in The Virgin Islands. Spencer held Carmen's hand in the taxicab as they rode to their hotel. He whispered, "I can't wait to feel your naked body against mine. AAAAAAAAAAHHHHHHHHH, I have waited for this too long." He kissed her forehead. She noticed his cock was getting extremely hard. "UUUUUUUUUMMMMMMMMMMM," he placed her hand on his throbbing cock. He rested his head against the back of the taxicab seat while she rested her head closely to his chest. They arrived at the hotel. After the bellboy left their room, he walked over and said, "At Last! We are alone." He slowly caressed her body; I want to embrace you in my arm and never let you go. "SSSSSSSSSHHHHHH, I waited for this moment for so long." He escorted her over to the bed; lets relax before going out to explore the Islands. Carmen, we both need a break from our busy lifestyle. Carmen, you are always so busy, and I can sense that it's extremely difficult for you to make time for yourself.

He massaged her body. He whispered, "I want to make your body relax. "UUUUUUMMMM." Spencer, that's what I need. My body hasn't relaxed in months. Carmen, you really must learn to slow down. He slowly massaged her neck. She moaned, "UUUUUUUUUUMMMMMMMMMMM, AAAAAAAAAAAHHHHHHHHHHHHH, YEEEEEEEEEEEEESSSSSSSS. Spencer, your hands feel SOOOOOOOOOOOOOO GOOOOOOOOOOOOD." He forcefully massaged his hand down her back as she closed her eyes. Her body began to relaxed as he slowly caressed his hand back and forth over her ass. He slid his hands down too her legs and feet. She moaned, "AAAAAAAAHHHHHHHHHHHHHHHH, EEEEEEEEERRRRRRRRR." She rolled over onto her back as he slowly massaged her breast. He kissed her breast as she rubbed his back. She moaned and groaned, "AAAAAAAHHHHHHHHHHHH; Spencer don't stop!" He moved his head in circular motions as he sucked her nipples. She slowly moved her ass back and forth on the bed as she whispered, "SSSSSSSHHHHHH, yes Spencer!" He slid his tongue down her stomach to her pussey. He licked her thighs. She was getting so excited until she took her hand and led his head down to her pussey. "OOOOOOOOOHHHHHHHHHHHHHH, Spencer, I want you to lick my pussey." He rubbed his tongue back and forth on her clit. She whispered, "Don't stop, your tongue feels WOOOOOONNNNNNDDDEEEEER." Spencer moaned, "AAAAAAHHHH, your pussey taste incredible. EEEEEEEERRRRRRRRRR, SSSSSSSSSSSSSSSSHHHHHHHHHH."

Spencer stopped licking her pussey and removed his pants and shirts. His cock was fat, thick and long. "UUUUUUUUUUUUUMMMMMMMMM," exactly the way she likes it. "My, my, my, Spencer your cock is huge. AAAAAAAAAHHHHHHH, I don't know if I can take all of it." Baby, sure you can – please relax. He raised her legs placing them over his shoulder. He slowly slid his cock into her pussey. "AAAAAAAAAAAHHHHHHHHHH, Spencer, your cock is TOOOOOOOOOOOO big OOOOOOOOOOOOHHHHHHHHH. Gosh! Stop now Spencer; your cock is hurting my pussey. UUUUUUUMMMMMMMMMMMMMM, SSSSSSSSSSHHHHHHHHHH, your cock is too big for my pussey." He kissed her cheeks please relax and enjoy my cock. I know you want it! I promise, I won' t hurt you, Carmen. He moved his ass extremely fast while he slid his cock in and out of her pussey. He moaned and groaned, "SSSSHHH, OOOOOOOOHHHHHHH, Baby your pussey is HOOOOOT. UUUUUUMMMM, I love the way your pussey is making my cock throb. OOOOOOOOOHHHHHHHHHHHHHH, YEEEEEEEEESSSSSSSS Carmen, my cock is so hard. I want to fuck you until you scream for more." She moaned, "YEEEEEEEEEEESSSSSSSSSSS Spencer, your cock feels as wonderful as it looks. UUUUUUUUUUUUMMMMMMMMM, AAAAAAAAAAAAAAAAAAAAAAAAHH, Baby your cock is making me CUUUUMMMM. AAAAAAAHHHH." Carmen, your pussey is, "SOOOOOOOOOOOO hot. Gosh Carmen! Your pussey feels SOOOOOOOOOOOOO tight! Carmen Baby, I'm CUUMMIIINNNGGG. AAAAAAAAAHHHHHHHHHHH. Gosh Baby!

Your pussey feels GOOOOOOOOOOOOD. SSSSSSSSHHHHHHHHHHHHHHHH, I'm CUUUUMMMMIIINNNGGG my hot load in shit Baby! I'm CUUUUMMIIIIIINNNNGG." He moved his cock faster and faster into her pussey. He yelled, "Shit Carmen! Don't stop moving your ass, please make me CUUUUUUMMMMMMM. Make me shoot my hot load into your pussey." He screamed, "EEEEEEEEEEEEEEEEEERRRRRRR, SSSSSSSSSSSSSSSHHHHHHHHHHH, YEEEEEEEEEEESSSSSSSSSSSS." His body shook as he came. He held her incredibly tight in his arm as he laid on her. She moaned, "OOOOOOOOOOOHHHHH Spencer. You are getting heavy; I can barely catch my breath." He softly laughed. "I'm sorry." He rolled over taking her into his arm until they both fell asleep.

When she awoke, she began unpacking her luggage. He awoke and asked, "What are you doing?" I thought I would unpack our luggage. She asked him; "Where are your keys?" Thanks Baby, my keys are in pants pocket. He rested in bed watching her as she unpacked their things. When she was done, he said, "I noticed; it's extremely difficult for you to relax." Yes, it is Spencer! Baby, I will teach you how to relax. She got back into bed. He advised her; I very seldom have much time, but I always find time to relax. "Baby, I can relax my ass off and trust me Carmen when you learn to relax your life will never be the same." He firmly caressed her arm; knowing when and how to relax is a gift.

He leaned on his elbow. Carmen, you are always so busy until you miss out appreciating the smaller things in life. Such as taking walks on the beach, walking in serene wooded areas, smelling flowers, listening to people's laughter, chirping birds, and the list goes on. When was the last time you walked on the beach? She chuckled; I can't recall Spencer. He whispered, "Try finding time for these things. Your business is doing well. Find time to create everlasting memories. Baby, we all want and need love. I know you possibly will say; "You don't want or need love, but love will make your life more complete. Love is such a beautiful thing." If love is so beautiful Spencer, "Why aren't you in love?" He let know her that he had fallen in love with her. Carmen, I fell in love with you the first night we met. I knew then, I wanted to spend the rest of my life with you.

The night you left with Jack, I was planning to walk you out to your car. But, Harper was much quicker than me. He left Karen in the restaurant for about an hour, and she still managed to have an awesome time. Spencer, please don't mention Jackson's name anymore while we're here on this trip. I want Jackson out of my life indefinitely. I have heard enough of his name. Okay, I promise Jackson will not be mentioned any more on this trip. She rubbed his chest and said, "You are right, I do want and need love but you can't hurry love." Liz has asked me on numerous occasions when am I planning to meet that special someone. She tells me; "I have been too busy playing match maker for my friends, until I have neglected getting into a wholesome relationship."

"Carmen do you remember when I shopped at Boshae` years ago?" She shook her head. Yes, I do and you are as sexy then as you are now! Well Carmen, I was constantly buying fur coats, leather outfits, and evening dresses for women trying to make them love me, and it only turned out to be artificial love. During that time, I asked Liz about you, and she said, "You were sorting things out in your personal life and wasn't interested in starting a new relationship". Yes! I instructed Liz to inform you and anyone else inquiring about my personal status that I wasn't interested in starting a new relationship. She sighed, "Spencer, I thought you were another man chasing behind many different women or vise-verse. You were always in a different relationship until I thought you were trying to see how many pussies you could fuck." He laughed and rolled over onto his stomach and kissed her. She rubbed her hand through his hair. "His brown body was SOOOOOOOOOOO well built and sexy. His body appeared as if he spent hours in the gym structuring it into a perfect physic."

He slid his tongue down her stomach and caressed it back and forth over her clit. Baby, I can't get enough of eating your pussey. "AAAAAAAHHHHHHHHHHHH, your pussey is SOOOOOOOOOOOOO tasty." He slid his tongue firmly against her clit while he fucked her with his finger. She slid her ass back and forth on the bed moaning and groaning, "AAAAAHHHH, UUUUUUUMMMMMM." She came all over Spencer's tongue. "AAAAAAAAAAHHHHHH, Baby, see what happens when you learn to relax your body." He kissed her pussey and said, "It doesn't take hours to cum when you learn the, "Art of relaxation." Baby, lets shower and walk out on the beach. Sure Spencer. They shower and changed into their swimsuit. Carmen put on her beach wrap, and they headed off to the beach. The air was crisp and fresh. The sunshine was bright and hot. The warm sand beneath their feet was comforting. The laughter of people echoed the air. The water was crystal blue. She divulged; "The serenity of the beach causes a state of tranquility. It really creates a relaxing state of mind." He kissed her and said, "Lets layout and relax on the beach, so we can enjoy the fresh air, the sounds of the wave and the laughter of people walking by. Carmen, these are the things we can appreciate. "AAAAAAAAAAHHHHHHHHHH, these are everlasting memories."

He rubbed his index finger back on forth on her arm; how many clothes can you buy, cars, houses, and material possession? Carmen, you can lose all material possessions at a drop of a hat, but memories can never be taken away. She listened intensely to him because she knew; he was making so much sense. He told her to close her eyes and envision something extremely pleasant. She closed her eyes. He asked her, "What was the first thing came to your mind?" Lying on the beach with you. He kissed her forehead. "AAAAAAAHHHHHHH!"

Now visualize another pleasant thing. He whispered, "Carmen share your thoughts with me." Spencer, I'm thinking about the pleasures of being free of worries. Being at peace with my inner thoughts. Great Carmen! Imagine of something else. Okay. Spencer, I'm thinking about falling in love with you. "SSSSSSSSSSHHHHHH, spending the rest of my life with you." He moaned, "UUUUUMMMM, Carmen, that's a great thought. Lets make that a reality."

Carmen, if you had one wish – what would you wish for? Gosh Spencer, that's an extremely difficult question. No Carmen! What would you wish for? "HHHHHHHHHMMMMMMMMM," let me see. I would wish to fall in love with a man that I could truly love, respect, communicate openly and honestly with him, and most of all – to build a strong committed relationship on a solid foundation of trust, integrity and strong ethical values. He whispered, "Carmen keep your eyes closed. You have been granted one wish; what is your granted wish?" Gosh Spencer, I don't know. He whispered, "Sure you know." She exhaled; "I have been granted an extremely peaceful lifestyle." He confidently asked, "How would it be peaceful?" Well Spencer for starters, I would no longer carry other people's burdens, and I would no longer care what's being thought about me. Also, I would find ways to bring happiness in my life without feeling I must make everyone else happy. Thanks Spencer! I have never taken the time to identify my wishes.

Carmen, "What do you daydream mostly about? She sighed, "I daydream about expanding Boshae`." He asked, "Why do you desire expanding Boshae`." Gosh! To increase Boshae` profit margin and that would undoubtedly, increase my clientele. Carmen, "If you had never opened Boshae` what profession would you be in today?" Spencer, I don't know. Baby, allow your imagination to flow. "What would your profession be today?" Spencer, "Possibly a schoolteacher." Come on Baby, let's go back into the room. If you like, we can come back out on the beach later tonight to watch the sunset. Before, we go into the room lets stop by and get a bucket of ice. She asked, "Ice!" He responded, "Yes, a bucket of ice!"

When they entered the room, Spencer set the bucket of ice on the table and took her into his arms and said, "I'm your student teach me something about the ice." She repeated, "Teach you something about the ice." Yes Baby, "If I was your student, and you were my teacher what lesson might I learn from you on the subject of ice!" He kissed her and whispered, "You have been granted a wish to become a schoolteacher for a day." Carmen stared deeply into his eyes and knew she has never met a man who has truly taken the time to know and understand her. She carried the bucket of ice over too the nightstand. She removed his swim trunk and said, "Get into bed!" She removed a piece of ice from the bucket and rubbed the ice over his lips. The ice was melting and running down his mouth. She kissed the water from his mouth. She slowing rubbed the ice down his body. His body shivered from excitement. He whispered, "AAAAAHHHHHHH teacher that feels goods." She took the ice and cupped it into her hand. She places her hand around his cock and firmly stroked it with the ice into of her hand. "EEEEEEERRRRRR, he moaned as he slid his cock back and forth in hands."

He rose up in bed moaning and groaning, "AAAAAAAHHHHHHHHHH. Teacher. You are teaching me an exceptionally WOONDERFUL lesson. AAAAAAAAAHHHHHHHHHHHHH, teacher don't stop!" Carmen took the ices and slowly rubbed it on his balls while she sucked his cock. "OOOOOOOOOHHHHHHHHHHH, teacher your mouth feels SOOOOOOOOOOO, damn, GOOOOOOOOOOOOOOOOOOOOOOD. AAAAAAAAAAAAAAAAHHHHHHHHHHHHHHHHH, I want to fuck your pussey." She slid her hands over his chest. He screamed, "AAAAHHH" as she sucked his cock with a piece of ice in her mouth. AAAAAAAAAAAAAAAAAHHHHHHHHHH, shit teacher, your lesson is GOOOOOOOOOD. AAAAAAAAAAAAAAAAAAHHHHHHHHHHHH, teacher can I be excused from this lesson? AAAAAAAAAAAAHHHHHHHHHHHHH, OOOOOOOOOHHHHHHHHHHHHHH. I'm CUUUUMMMMMMMMIIIINNGG right now. I don't want to cum this fast. UUUUUMMMMMMMM, teacher will I fail if I CUUUUUUUUUMMMMMMMMMMM. AAAAAAAAAAAAHHHHHHHHHHHHHHHHH. Damn teacher, he was getting louder and louder. AAAAAAAAAAAHHHHHHH, teacher, I'm CUUUUMMMMMMMMIIIIIINNGG. She stopped and placed a piece of ice in her pussey. She sat on his cock. He moaned, "EEEEEEERRRRRRRRRRRRRRRRRRRR." He screamed, "UUUUUUUUUUUMMMMM, I'm CUUUUMMMMIIINNNGGG." He kissed her forehead and said, "With imagination, it is easy to conquer anything in life." She rubbed his chest and said, "Yes Spencer, that's so true!"

He suggested; "Let shower and go downstairs to the restaurant for dinner and a few drinks." They showered and went downstairs. After dinner, Spencer complimented the chef and said, "It would be great if you relocated back to Seattle." The chef replied, "Let me get back with you."

Baby, Lets go into the lounge and have a few drinks. He ordered a Hennessy on the rocks and a Martini for Carmen. He acknowledged; I knew we would be together from the first day; I met you. She admitted to him that she wasn't extremely thrilled about coming to his restaurant on the night they met, but I'm extremely happy – I did! She suggested, "First thing in the morning, why don't we explore the Islands." He smiled, if you would like, but I would prefer spending this time with you away from everyone. "SSSSSSSHHHHHH, keeping you all for myself is what I truly desire."

After finishing their drinks, they headed upstairs. Baby lets lie in bed and embrace each other tonight. They undressed and got into bed. She rested in his arms as the moonlight shunned into the window against his hard cock. He whispered, "UUUUUUMMMMMMMMMMMMM Baby, the moonlight is extremely bright tonight." Yes Spencer! The moonlight is bright. He sighed, "The moonlight is something worth appreciating." She didn't respond. As he promised, he held her in his arms all night. They slept in late, awakening feeling ever so refreshed. They showered and spent the remaining of the day exploring the Islands. Each day, Spencer and Carmen ventured into another part of the Islands appreciating the breath taking beauty of all the sceneries Mother Nature offered them. They were like kids exploring and experiencing the native's cultures. He raved about how exquisite the Islands are! He said, "It sadden me that our vacation will eventually come to an end. I have really enjoyed spending this time with you. Not too mention, all the great places; we've toured since being here on the Islands." They returned too the hotel. Carmen said, "Lets have an early dinner and go out on the beach. I have never spent Christmas Eve out on the beach nor Christmas day." Sure Carmen! This will be a precious memory to create for us.

They returned to their room and changed into their swimwear and went out on the beach. He whispered, "What did you tell Santa Clause you wanted for Christmas?" Mr. Goodman, I asked Santa Clause to bring me an extremely tall, dark, and handsome man. Carmen, "Do you believe Santa will deliver it?" "Yes! Santa delivered my gift earlier this year." She kissed Spencer. "So Carmen, what is your opinion about Santa's gift?" It's the best gift; I have ever received for Christmas. She yelled out loud, "Thank you Santa." Spencer sat up and said, "Come here Carmen." He hugged her and said, "I wish I could hug you like this forever and never let you go." She whispered, "Be very careful what you wish for Santa – may possibly deliver it." "UUUMMMM, Carmen lets go back to the room, so we can make love tonight." He said, "Baby, I want to feel my cock sliding into your pussey." Shit, I want more and more of you each day.

He removed her swimsuit as she relaxed in bed. He knelt on his knees sliding his hard throbbing cock into her wet pussey. He began moaning, "SSSSSSSSSSSSSSSSSHHHHHHHHHHHH, UUUUUUMMMMMMMMMMMMMMMM, as soon as his cock entered her pussey. EEEEEEERRRR, your pussey it hot and tight. AAAAAAAAAHHHHHH, Shit Baby! Your pussey fit my cock like a glove. UUUUUUUUMMMMMMMMMMMMMMMM, EEEEEEEEERRRRRR, your pussey really is turning me on." He raised her legs over his shoulder as he slid his cock faster and faster into her hot and wet pussey. She slid her ass back and forth on the bed as she got into her fuck groove. He whispered, "AAAAAAAAAAAAAAAAHHHHHHHHHHH, I'm so glad we met. I'm shooting my load into your pussey. AAAAAAAAAAAAHHHHHH, Carmen don't stop moving your ass! I want your pussey to make me CUUUUUUUUMMMMMMMMMM. SSSSSSSSSSSSSSSSSSHHHHHHHHH, AAAAAAAAAAAAAAAHHHHHHHHH, I'm CUUUUMMMMIIIIIINNNGGGGG. SSSSSSSSSSSSSSSSHHHHHHHHHHH, EEEEEEEEEEERRRRRRRRRRRRRRRRRRR, MMMMMMMMMMMMMMMMMMMMMM, your pussey felt incredible." He felt as if he was losing control as he kissed her. His heart was pounding against his chest. His mind was racing with many thoughts. His body jerked as sweat rolled down his forehead. He moaned and groaned to the top of his voice, "AAAAAAAAAAAHHHHHHHHH, UUUUUUUUUUUUMMMMMMMM. Carmen, I love you." She thought, "Please don't rush things."

The day finally arrived for them to leave the Islands. Prior to leaving the hotel, she thanked him for the wonderful time. She later said, "I can't remember when I've had so much fun." Carmen, I'm glad; you had a wonderful time. I promise, we will have more times like this. He hugged her; I would like to escort you to, "The New Year's Eve Bash at my restaurant." Yes Spencer! There is no one else in this world I would rather bring the New Year's in with. Prior to leaving the room, he held her hands extremely firmly and kissed her. He said, "I wish this vacation didn't have to end so quickly." She stared into his eyes. Thanks! I truly needed this vacation.

As they flew back to Seattle, Carmen closed her eyes and thought, "This was the best time, I've had in a long time, but it's time to get, "Back to reality."

Chapter Ten

Back To Reality

They arrived in Seattle around noonish. He carried her luggage into her house and said, "I will call you later this evening." She briefly sat on her couch and decided to drive over too the boutique to help Liz, since the, "Holiday Season" is the most hectic time of the year. When she entered the boutique, Liz greeted her – welcome back Carmen. "How was your vacation?" Liz, it was fantastic. Spencer is so much fun and not to mention – exceedingly adventurous. The time, I spent with him is what I really needed and deserved. We did more talking than anything. Liz, Spencer has a way with engaging in great conversations. He was really genuine in wanting to know me better. He has taught me the true "Art of relaxation." I had time to strategize a new business plan for the boutique and also to make personal goals for the New Year's.

She took a deep breath. Liz, "How was business?" Carmen, business was great, although, Jackson stopped by the boutique at least fifty times. Come on Liz. Trust me Carmen, he did. "So what did you tell him?" Carmen, what else should I have told him other than you were out of town. Liz, did he ask where I was? Yes Carmen! He did and through his art of persuasion; I told him your destination. He promised he wouldn't fly there. Liz, I'm surprise that you are so weak when it comes to Jackson Harper. Gosh Carmen! Jackson is so savvy in his approach. It almost feels as his eyes can pierce one's soul. Whenever, I talk with Jackson I feel totally connected to him. Carmen sighed, "Yes Liz, I know exactly what you mean! He sometimes influences me the same way."

Sorry Carmen, but Jackson has a way with words. At first he said, he was flying there to see you, but I told him not to waste his time or money. I told him; you were on vacation with Spencer, and he became outrageously furious. He took his hand and brushed everything off the counter over by the register onto the floor. "Were there any clients in the shop?" No! But, I don't believe it would have made any difference with him. He was furious, and it appeared; he didn't give a damn about anything. He said, "He couldn't believe; you flew out of town without letting him know." Liz, Jackson has lost his mind if he assume; I will allow him to dictate my personal life. I'm sure I will hear all about his concerns when I see him. Carmen, I told him you would be back late tonight, so look forward to hearing from him. Liz, I had a wonderful time, but I knew it would all end once the plane landed; I would be "Back in reality." Liz, I really didn't want to return, but of course, Spencer needed to return to his business and likewise with me.

Oh Carmen, Mr. Jenkins called on several occasion asking about you. Liz, I hope you didn't tell him where I went. No! Jackson is the only one who knew you were out of town. "HHHHHHHHHMMMMMMMMMMMM," okay, Liz, I will call Mr. Jenkins when I have enough time. "So what else happened while I was gone? Did you make any plans for the wedding?" Yes! Melvin and I purchased the wedding dress; it's quite lovely. We've made plans to have an outside garden wedding at my home. Liz, your wedding will be extremely lovely since your garden is magnificent. Melvin has placed his home on the market. "Why Liz?" He said, "He liked my house plan much better." Now Liz, you should consider Melvin keeping his home as rental property. Carmen, there seems to be no problem with our future plans. Yea Liz, I'm extremely happy for you. "Did many ladies stopped by to purchase evening gowns for the New Year's Eve Bash at Spencer's?"

Gosh Carmen! It has been incredible in the boutique. The sales have been off-the hook.

Tell me Carmen, "How was your Christmas in the Virgin Islands?" It was magnificent! Spencer and I relaxed on the beach; this was a first for the both of us. You look great Carmen! Thanks Liz, I got plenty of rest. Something, I was lacking abundance of. "So Liz, what do you and Melvin have planned for New Year's Eve?" Liz smiled. Spencer's restaurant will be the social gathering for everyone on New Year's Eve.

Carmen, Shirley and Jason stopped by to see you while you were gone. You wouldn't believe it, but they were married in Las Vegas. Liz, when did this take happen? I didn't get all of the details, but they seemed extremely happy. "What about Jessie?" I heard through the grapevine he's seeing a twenty-five year old lady with two small children. Liz, lets hope this young lady knows what she has gotten herself into. I don't believe Jessie will stay around for a reasonably long time. Particularly, since he doesn't have children of his own. I truly believe; he doesn't like children. Now Carmen, that's none of your business so stay out of Jessie and his lady friend business. Yes Liz! I will mind my business, but I fell really sorry for his lady friend. Carmen, please mind your own business. Liz, those are my plans.

Oh Carmen, I have been keeping the boutique open this entire week until 8:00 P.M. and on Saturday;

I have closed at 4:00 P.M. Great Liz! That's a wonderful plan but don't spend too much time at the boutique and most importantly don't neglect your time with Melvin. I know Carmen, but the clientele asked, "Me to keep the boutique open later this week?" Okay, Liz, I'm going home now; it seems; you have everything under control. I need to open my mail and wind down.

The phone ranged. Excuse me Carmen; I will get that. Hello. No Jackson! She has left for home. You might try reaching her at home. Bye-Liz, I will see you in the morning. Goodnight Carmen! When Carmen arrived home, she called Spencer postponing their dinner commitment for a later date in the week. Prior to calling him, she listened to her message and was extremely surprised; she received a message from him. Hello Carmen, I really want to see you. It's extremely urgent! I have not been totally honest sharing my personal life with you. Please stop by the restaurant as soon as possible. It's awfully important; I will explain everything to you when you get here. I'm looking forward to seeing you tonight. Carmen, I'm truly sorry about everything. Bye.

She thought, "Gosh! He sounds upset. What could he possibly want to tell me? As she poured water for a cup of tea, the phone ranged. Hello. Hi Carmen, it's Jackson. Hi Jackson, I'm doing really well. "How are things with you and Karen?" Carmen, we are doing well. "So, why are you calling me if you and Karen are doing so well!" Carmen, "What's with the attitude?" Oh, me Jackson, I don't have an attitude. Jackson, "Why are you calling me?" I want to hear everything about your vacation! "My vacation?" Yes Carmen! I just left Spencer and found out that you and he flew to the Virgin Islands for a romantic vacation. No Jackson, you didn't just found out! Liz told you while I was away. "Now Jackson! Why aren't you minding your own business? And, what have you told Spencer about us?" Nothing Carmen. Jackson, the truth! What have you said to Spencer? I casually spoke with Spencer and told him that I haven't seen him in the restaurant within the past two weeks and where have he been? Jackson, why do you feel you need to know everything? You seem to feel; it's okay to interfere in my relationships. You called Jessie. Yes Carmen! I called Jessie, and he turned out to be a rotten son of a bitch. I heard, he is –stop it Jackson! I don't want to hear that nonsense from you. Jackson, I already know. Liz has already shared the news with me. "How is Karen?" She is doing magnificent, Carmen! "What are you and Karen doing on New Year's Eve?" We have made reservation at Spencer's. "What about you Carmen, are you planning to toast in the New Year's with your new lover boy?" Jackson, you will have to wait and see. "Jackson, what is this nonsense about you getting so angry that you took your hands and brushed everything off my countertop?" Oh Carmen, that was an accident. Carmen, can I see you tonight, since I haven't seen you in two weeks? No Jackson! I'm spending tonight with Spencer. "Damn! Carmen, haven't you spent enough time with him!" No Jackson, I haven't! Carmen, that son of a bitch is separated from his wife. No Jackson, Spencer isn't married! He has never been married, nor does he have any children. The hell, he isn't married or doesn't have any children. Carmen, Spencer has been married for ten years. He has been separated for three of those years. Jackson, that explains everything! Spencer left a message on my answering machine telling me that he hasn't been totally truthful about his personal life. He said, "He needs to share this information immediately." "Don't tell me Jackson; you have threaten Spencer. Now, he has no choice but to share everything with me now." Damn! Carmen reflect back, hasn't it been three years, since Spencer shopped at Boshae`.

Carmen, what did Spencer tell you? Did he tell you; he's single and that he doesn't have any children? Yes, he did Jackson, but why are you so angry! Carmen if you are falling for Spencer because you thinks he's single; you are sadly mistaken. Spencer is married and also has a daughter five-year-old. Tears rolled from her eyes. Damn Jackson, I don't believe you. "Why are you lying to me?" Carmen, I drew up legal documents for Spencer to legally separate from his estranged wife. "Gosh Jackson! It seem as if I don't know Spencer at all! Why are you trying to prevent me from starting a relationship with him." Because Carmen, he's not being truthful with you. Carmen, when I first met you, "Didn't I tell you; I was married." He yelled, "Didn't I tell you; I had three grown children? Didn't I tell you; I was married to Karen over thirty years, and I didn't love her, but I'm will not divorce her?" Jackson, don't act as if you are so perfect and that you haven't done anything wrong. Carmen, our affair was wrong, but I never deceived you. Yes Jackson! You told me all of those things, but it was still wrong for us to have an affair.

Jackson, I don't believe Spencer has deceived me; I really need to hear his version of this story. As far as I'm concern, he's single until I hear those exact words from his mouth. Bullshit Carmen, he has deceived you! Spencer is married, and he has refused to divorce his estranged wife. Jackson, how do you know Spencer has refused divorcing his estranged wife? Did you ask him to divorce his wife? "Answer me Jackson!" Yes Carmen! I asked Spencer whether he needed an attorney to draw up his divorce decreed, and he declined my offer. He became outraged and asked me to leave his office. Jackson, as outraged as, you are now! Carmen, I'm only proving a point that Spencer is a liar and a cheat. She sighed, "Precisely, like you Jackson!"

He was becoming extremely irritated by her attitude. He forcefully said, "Carmen, I will stop by your home in twenty minutes – now be there!" No Jackson, I'm getting dressed to drive over to Spencer's! "What do you expect for him to tell you?" Jackson, I expect the truth! I want to hear everything from Spencer's mouth and not yours. Jackson, when will you mind your business? Carmen, you are my business and don't ever forget. Sadly, you believe that Jackson! But, I really believe you should focus your attention on Karen. You will be better off that way. Bye-Jackson, I need to shower. Carmen, I will be over in twenty minutes. Jackson stay away from my home. Bye.

Carmen stepped from the shower and heard the doorbell ranged? She checked the monitor. There stood Jackson. She asked, "Jackson why are you here and what do you want?" Carmen, I need to talk with you. Okay Jackson! I will open the door, but you only have fifteen minutes. She opened the door with a towel wrapped around her body. Hi Carmen, I really missed you. Hi Jackson. He moaned, "AAAAAHHHHH. Start talking Jackson. You only have fifteen minutes." Come here Carmen. He tried hugging her, but she said, "Not now Jackson." She stared into his eyes and asked, "Why are you so angry?"

He walked over and hugged her extremely tight. He caressed his hands over her body. She whispered, "UUUUUUUMMM, please tell me why you are here?" He kissed her vigorously. "AAAAHHHHH, because I missed you at the same time you were gone. I wanted to see you so damn badly. SSSSSSSSSSSHHHHHHHHHHHHHHH, UUUUUUUMMMMMMMMMMMM, Carmen, you smell SOOOOOOOOOOOOOOO GOOOOOOOOOOOOOOOOOOOOOOD, AAAAAAAAAAAAHHHHHHHHHH," he rubbed his hard cock against her body. She whispered, "UUUUUUUUUUUUUUUMMMMMMM, Jackson, your cock is SOOOOOOOOOOOOO hard."

"YEEEEESSSS Carmen. SSSSSSSSHHHH, my cock has been throbbing since you left town. I have been yearning to fuck you every night with my hard throbbing cock. Hell! I wanted to feel my cock stroking your hot pussey since you left town. AAAAAAAAAHHHHHHHHH, he kissed her neck." Her breathing was getting louder and louder as he slid his tongue over tits. He muscularly sucked on her nipples. She moaned and groaned as she ran her fingers through his hair. The phones ranged. AAAAAAAAAAAAHHHHHHHHHHH, shit don't answer it; let it ring! Jackson, I need to answer the phone. Hello, Hi, Spencer. Yes, I'm planning to stop by the restaurant later today! "Why do you ask whether; I have talked with Jackson?" He hesitated; "Well, have you Carmen?" Yes Spencer, I have talked with Jackson! He has shared some extremely alarming information about your personal life. "Please Carmen, can I see you right now?" Sure Spencer, I will stop by within the next hour. Jackson is still here. "Carmen, what is it with Jack?" She asked, "What do you mean?" He furiously said, "Why is he so angry that you and I were on vacation together?" Spencer, I don't know, but I will ask him and tell you later. Bye-Spencer.

Jackson stepped closer to Carmen. No Jackson, not now! I must get dressed. Spencer is waiting to see me. He whispered, "The hell with Spencer, I want you now." He kissed her and held her, "SOOOOOOOOOOOOOOOO tightly." He knelt down on the floor in the foyer. He removed the towel from her body as he slid his tongue back and forth over her stomach. "AAAAAHHHHHHH, I missed holding you in my arms." He asked her to lie on the floor as he slid his tongue over her wet clit. "AAAAAAAAAAAAHHHHH, Carmen, I miss eating your pussey." She moaned, "SSSSHHHHH, don't stop Jackson. Your tongue feels SOOOOOO wonderful." He began sliding his finger back and forth in her pussey as he licked her clit. "AAAAAAAAAAAAAHHHHHHHHHHH,

Carmen, I want you so badly. My cock is so hard until it feels is if it will explode. AAAAAAAHHHHH shit Carmen!" The phone ranged again. Shit Carmen! Let it pick up on the answering machine.

The voice came on. Hi Carmen. It's Randolph Jenkins. I really would like to see you. I have another great idea; I would like to share with you. I want to embrace you in my arms and make love to you the way I did, "At the Cabin." Jackson became furious! Who the hell is that Carmen? I know you didn't fuck Randolph Jenkins. "Jackson, did he mentioned anything about fucking?" Carmen, he said, "He wanted to embrace you in his arm and make love to you. When the hell were you at his cabin?" Carmen picked the towel from the floor and wrapped it around her body. She opened the door and said, "Jackson, get the hell out of my home." Prior to leaving her house he said, "Your deceitfulness will one day cause you enormous pain." She closed the door and went upstairs, dressed and drove over to the restaurant.

She walked into the restaurant requesting to see Spencer. The Waitress escorted her to his office. She stood by his desk. He said, "Hug me Carmen." She didn't respond. He stood from his chair. Do you mind if I closed the door? No, I don't mind at all Spencer! I know; Jackson has already shared with you that I'm married and have a five-year-old daughter. Yes Carmen! This is true! But, I'm not in love with my wife. Spencer, I don't want to hear that bullshit because if you don't love her, why haven't you divorced her years ago. Frankly, I've heard enough of your lies. By the way Spencer, "Who is your estrange wife?" Robin Spencer. She sighed, "Oh, Becky Flowers sister." Yes Carmen! Robin would have tried her best to rob me blind if I divorced her. She's a gold digger. I should have known this when I first met her. Robin's entire conversation revolved around money and the things money could buy for her, and it sicken me. Carmen, when Robin moved out, she spent money without considerations for future investments. After analyzing the situation, I requested Jack drew up legal separation documents. Jackson recommended that I award Robin twenty-five percent of my business. I told Jack, "Hell no! It's cheaper to stay married to Robin." She stared at him with skepticism, "Boy, have I heard that so many times." Believe it Carmen! It is the honest truth! Carmen, "Why is Jack Harper so concern with your personal life? His behavior focuses me to believe that you two are in a "Forbidden love affair." No Spencer! Jackson is no more than a really good friend. I have sought legal advice from him, now he thinks; he must look out for my best interests. Spencer, you must remember that Jackson is well known throughout the community. Yes Carmen! But, I don't understand why the hell he keeps asking me whether; I have slept with you or not? Spencer, that is none of Jackson's damn business, and you should make him understand that.

Carmen, I hope you are stilling planning to attend the New Year's Eve Bash? She shrugged her shoulders; I don't know for sure, but I will try my best. I'm getting awfully tired, so I'm leaving now. I will call you tomorrow. Spencer, have a goodnight. She hugged him prior to leaving the restaurant.

Chapter Eleven

Ready For The New Year's

Carmen was awakened on New Year's Eve morning debating with herself whether she would attend the New Year's Eve Bash at Spencer's. She thought, "I've had enough drama for one year. I will stay at home and watch the New Year's Eve celebration on television." She moaned, "UUUUUUUUUUUUUUUMMMMMMMM, YEEEEEEESSSSSS," I will write out my New Year's resolutions.

At 10:30 A.M., she called Liz wishing Melvin and her a happy and very prosperous New Year's. Liz, if I don't attend the bash at Spencer's tonight please, you and Melvin have a grand time. Gosh Carmen! You sound as if you have decided not to attend the big bash tonight at Spencer's. Carmen, is everything okay with you? Sure Liz, everything is okay.

Liz sighed, "Carmen, have you talked with Jackson?" Yes, I have and Jackson has shared some extremely alarming information about Spencer's personal life! "Liz, did you know; Spencer is married and has a daughter?" Yes Carmen! Jackson discussed this issue with me days ago. Liz, why didn't you tell me? Carmen, I thought Spencer should share this information with you, himself.

Liz, I'm surprised; Becky never mentioned that Robin has been married to Spencer over ten years. I have asked Becky about Robin on numerous occasions, and she would always respond, "If you only knew." Oh Carmen! Becky hasn't spoken to Robin, since Spencer proposed to her. "Why Liz?" Becky dated Spencer many years ago, and she became furious after Spencer married Robin. Bye-Liz, I have heard enough of this drama. Tell Melvin, I said, "Hello and Happy New Year's."

The doorbell ranged. Carmen opened the door and practically fainted upon seeing Karen standing at her door. She was extremely curious to find out the nature of Karen's visit. Hi Carmen, "Can, I please come in?" Sure Karen, come on in. Karen began crying. Carmen, Jack is home packing his clothing; he's leaving me. Carmen hastily asked, "Jackson is doing what?" He's packing his things, and said, "He needs breathing room." Karen, I don't believe; what you are telling me. Why the sudden change in

Jackson's behavior. Carmen, he said "He hasn't loved me for a while and needs time to sort things out." Gosh! Karen on New Year's Eve; I don't believe Jackson is telling you that he needs time away from you. The nerves of him! Karen cried. "Carmen, I'm so scared. Jack is the only man that I have ever loved. Hell Carmen, I have spent my entire life with Jack. What will I do without him in my life?" Carmen thought, "What the hell have I done?" Karen, did Jackson mention to you whether he's interested in anyone else? No Carmen! He hasn't mentioned seeing anyone, nor that he's interested in anyone. Karen, do you suspect anyone?" No Carmen! Jack has always spent his time with me when he's not at work or traveling. About nine months ago, I began noticing major changes in Jack. "What kind of changes Karen?" Carmen, for starters! "Jack asked me regularly to engage in threesomes with him. I have told him yes on many occasions, but he has never pursued bringing the third person home." Carmen listened intensely. Carmen, "Whenever I asked, "When was he planning to introduced me to the third person; he became enraged? He would later tell me that he was only testing my sexuality."

Carmen sighed, "Did Jackson say where he will be staying?" Karen glanced at Carmen; I was so upset until that question never crossed my mind. Carmen thought, "I sure in hell hope he doesn't believe; he's moving in with me." Karen, I will call Jackson to find out what triggered this episode. Hello Jackson! This is Carmen. Hi Baby, I'm leaving Karen today. I know Jackson; your wife is sitting in my living room. Jackson asked, "Did you tell Karen about us?" No Jackson! I didn't tell Karen about our affair and neither will you. Karen is extremely upset about your sudden plans to leave her. "Jackson, what has triggered this shift in your behavior?" Damn Jackson! It's New Year's Eve. This is really poor timing. Carmen, I want to spend my life with you. "Jackson are you listening to me? This is poor timing – it's New Year's Eve!" Carmen, why should I spend another year with someone that I don't love? Hell! I will not spend another day with Karen? Jackson, please stop this behavior.

No Carmen, I'm telling Karen about us! No Jackson, please don't! Carmen, I will not lie any longer to Karen. I don't take pleasure in being trapped in this "Web of lies, sex, and deceit." Carmen heart began beating out of control. She pleaded with him not to reveal their, "Forbidden Love Affair" to Karen. She cried out, "Lets talk first! Why don't you stop by my house?" No Carmen! Jackson, please stop by, so we can talk. Okay Carmen, but you will not change my mind about leaving Karen. Carmen glanced at Karen and said, "Do you mind leaving? Jackson is on his way here. I will at least try talking some sense into him?"

Karen smiled and said, "Thanks Carmen and walked out."

He ranged the doorbell. Hello Jackson, "Have you lost your mind?" I thought months ago; you were losing your mind, but today; you have proven that you have seriously lost your mind. Of all days Jackson, "Why are you choosing "New Year's Eve" to leave Karen?" Carmen, I don't want to start another New Year's with Karen pretending that I want to share the rest of my life with her. She is expecting to celebrate at Spencer's tonight with me. Hell Carmen! I want to spend tonight with you instead. Jackson, you cannot disappoint Karen on New Year's Eve. Hell Carmen! I won't be able to endure seeing you with your new lover tonight. No Jackson, you will not see me with Spencer tonight! I'm not celebrating at his restaurant. She sighed, "I will be celebrating at Michello` Eatery and Winery. So please escort your wife to his party." He hesitated; I will leave Spencer and meet you at Michello`. Okay Jackson, that sounds like an excellent plan! Now, call Karen and apologize to her. "Tell her that you were not thinking clearly and ask her to forgive you for being a total jerk on New Year's Eve. Also tell her that you were being insensitive toward her feelings." He dialed his home number. Karen, this is Jack, "Please hear me out. I don't know what came over me earlier today, but I want to apologize for being so insensitive. Please forgive me and trust me Karen;

this will never happen again. Karen, I love you and truly want you in my life. Baby, I will be home shortly." Bye-Jack!

Jackson walked over to Carmen and kissed her. She kissed him and said, "I haven't given you your Christmas gift." She went into the kitchen returning with a can of cool whip, a jar of cherries and a glass of ice. She escorted him by his hands upstairs to her bedroom. She removed his clothing and sprayed the cool whip on his cock placing two cherries on the head of his cock as it pointed straight into the ceiling. His breathing was out of control as he moaned and groaned, "EEEEEERRRRRRRRRRRRRRRRR, what are you doing to me? AAAAAAHHHHHH Carmen, this feels so GOOOOOOOOD." She slowly licked the cool whip from his cock and slid her body in bed until her mouth reached his mouth. She dropped a cherry into his mouth and slid her tongue into his mouth, so he could eat the cool whip. Oh Baby, please don't stop. I really like what you are doing to me. She ate the last cherry from his cock. His breathing was getting louder and louder. His hair was soaked from sweating. He screamed in an awfully strong and piercing voice, "AAAAAAHHHHH. Carmen, I'm SOOOOOOOOOOOOO excited." She removed the ice from the glass and cupped it inside her hands and began stroking his cock. He rose straight up in bed and said, "Carmen, I can't take this any longer. You are driving me crazy." She whispered, "Please relax." As she stroked his cock harder and faster with several pieces of ice in her hands, he moaned, "AAAAAAAHHHHHHHHHHHH, UUUUUUUMMMMMMMMMMMM." She stroked his cock faster and faster until he forcefully removed her hands away moaning, "NOOOOOOO Baby, I can't take anymore of this."

He slid his hard throbbing cock into her pussey moaning, "OOOOOOOOHHHHHHHHHHH, Carmen, please move your ass. I want to fuck you until you CUUUUUMMMMMMMMMM." His breathing was echoing the room as he kissed her lips. His body was dripping with sweat. "AAAHHHHHHHHHHH, I want to make you CUUUUUUUUUMMMMMMMMM." Carmen pussey was getting SOOOOOOOO wet. He moaned, "Shit Carmen! Your pussey is SOOOOO HOOOOOOOT." She whispered, "please remove your cock, so I can place ice into my pussey." He moaned, "SSSSSSSSSSHHHHHH, AAAAAAAAAAARRRRRRRRRRRRR, as he fucked her pussey with the ice. OOOOOOHHHHHHHHH shit Carmen, your pussey is SOOOO damn HOOOOOOOOOOT and it feels SOOOOOOOOOOO cold. AAAAAAAAAARRRRRRRRRRRRRRRRRR, UUUUMMMMMMMMMM, I have never fucked a pussey that felt SOOOOOOOOOOOOOO hot and cold at the same time, AAAAAAAAHHHHHHHH. I'm CUUUUMMMMMMIIIIINNNGGGG." When Jackson came, it seemed as if he shot his load into her pussey for hours. He hugged her extremely tight and whispered, "Thanks for the wonderful Christmas gift. I will always treasure this gift as a precious memory." She whispered, "Thanks Jackson; you should leave now! There's only a few hours before the celebration began at Spencer's tonight." After Jackson left, Carmen showered, unplugged her phone, and turned on the television to watch the New Year's Eve celebration. She closed her eyes and reflected back over the year, "I've had enough excitement for one year, but on the other hand; I'm looking forward to a "Blissful New Year's with Old Lovers." I'm definitely ready for the New Year's and all the prosperity it will bring.

www.ingramcontent.com/pod-product-compliance
Ingram Content Group UK Ltd.
Pitfield, Milton Keynes, MK11 3LW, UK
UKHW041848190726
13854UKWH00002B/773